Reign:

We See Him As He Is

David J. Keyser

ISBN: 978-0-615-25759-4

Foreword

It is very important for the reader to understand
that the author does not pretend to actually
describe in this book what the millennial reign will
be like or to predict the time for the beginning of
those 1,000 years. This is all fictional speculation,
a sort of "What if . . ." story based on one historic
position that there will be a literal reign for a
thousand years from Jerusalem which still lies in
our future.

Dedication

This book is dedicated to my wife, Judith. It is not
possible to communicate all the love,
encouragement and wisdom that she has given me.

Introduction

My name is Tim. I am the Keeper. I am the 15th generation from Mother Anna by direct succession. It is the year 999 C.R., almost a thousand years of the Emperor's reign. I have selected these excepts from the private journals of some of my predecessors in order to speak to the people of my time through them. I have also added two dates for each of my predecessors/ancestors; the date they took office and the date of their soul's passing beyond the great veil.

Definition: A Dais, or Dias, is an elevated place in a building or on the ground for speakers or important people to sit or stand on so that they can be better seen and heard by the surrounding crowd.

In a moment, in the twinkling of an eye, at
the last trump: for the trumpet shall sound,
and the dead shall be raised incorruptible,
and we shall be changed.
I Cor. 15:52

And they lived and reigned with Christ a
thousand years.
Rev.20:4

Do ye not know that the saints shall judge
the world?
I Cor.6:2

Reign: We See Him As He Is

Chapters:

Reign: We See Him As He Is

THE ANNATIC LINE

1. **Anna** was the mother of Mark

2. **Mark** was the father of Carl.

3. Carl was the father of Alice,

4. Alice was the mother of May.

5. **May** was the aunt of Orin

6. Orin was the father of James.

7. James was the father or Patricia.

8. Patricia was the mother of Andrew.

9. Andrew was the father of **Joan** and Marie

10. Marie was the mother of Mandie.

11. Mandie was the mother of Ken.

12. Ken was the father of Merle.

13. **Merle** was the mother of Kathryn

14. Kathryn was the mother of Sarah and Elizabeth

15. Elizabeth was the mother of **Tim** and she died in childbirth.

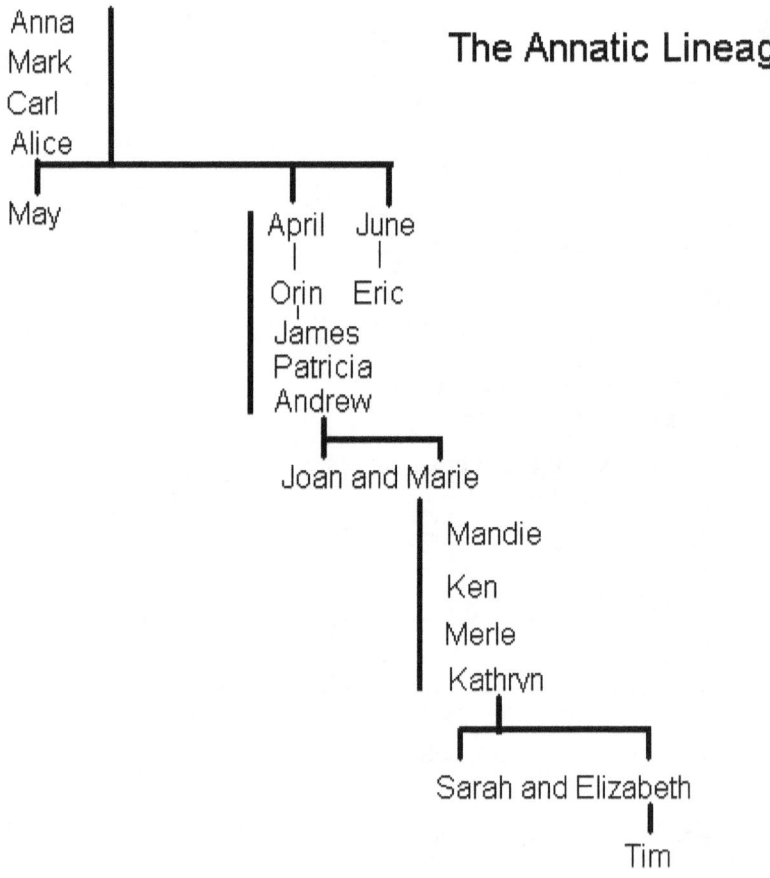

The Annatic Lineage

1 * ANNA

103 – 159 C.R.

04.14.103 C.R.   My name is Anna. I am the third of four daughters of John Semple of Buckhead. I have two older sisters, a younger sister and two younger brothers. John Jr. is directly below me, then Gracie, then the baby Seth. Vanessa is just older than I and Joan is the oldest. My father is the assistant administrator of Buckhead. My mother, Grace, is ten years younger than my father. He always says that he was fortunate to get her and they had to have children quickly to make up for the time he had wasted.

The year is 103 of the Glorious Reign under the great and righteous rule of His Imperial Majesty who rules from Jerusalem. My family is mortal and we do not despise our mortality although I am definitely the most curious one in my family regarding the Immortals. Our Immortals are especially kind. They never act haughty and are very considerate of us all. As a matter of fact, you might say that I am somewhat of a friend of our local Governor, the Immortal Elaine, who rules Buckhead.

I came to meet her Excellency, Elaine, in an unusual way. I was carrying my little niece, Alice, Joan's little girl, home from school one day as she had turned her ankle playing at school. The teacher said that it would mend if she stayed off of it for a while. She sent for me in the upper school (I have only one more year) so that I could carry her home. I was crossing a road near a turn when I heard the great beast approaching and I could not get myself and little Alice out of the way in time, so I threw us both on the ground and covered her with my body. The horse almost cleared me but I felt one hoof smash down on my left hip and heard it crack. The rider, a mortal like myself, did not stop. Some friends came along and carried me and little Alice home. I was hurting a lot. The physician was sent for.

Before the physician could arrive, Governor Elaine herself appeared at our home. My parents were shocked. What had we done? The Governor explained that she was there to look after me and they showed her to the room that I share with Vanessa and Gracie. I tried to rise but she motioned with her hand that I should stay still. "Well, young Anna, your hip is broken," she said.

"Yes, Excellency."

"Let's make it well. What do you say?"

"Yes, ah . . . I would be . . . most grateful." My voice trailed off at the end.

The broken hip was on the top side as I laid on my bed. My mother had already expressed a fear that I would always limp and would probably not be able to get a husband. She did not know that I had overheard. The Governor touched my hip lightly with her scepter. At first it felt warm, then it seemed to swell a little for a short time, then it cooled and the pain was gone. She bid me rise. I got up and was as whole as I had been before the accident. I had always known that they had this power but this was my first experience of it.

"There now. You feel fine now," she said.

"Yes, Excellency. Fine, thank you. Thank you so very much." I started to kneel
before her but she pulled me up.

"That's fine, girl," she said.

"You threw yourself on the child?" she asked.

"Yes, Excellency."

"A selfless act."

"I, I did not think," I responded.

"Yes," she smiled, "instinctive, and that girl, . . . speaks even better of you."

"Yes, er, I mean, thank you, Excellency." The Immortal Elaine, Governor of Buckhead and Vice-Metropolitan of Atlanta smiled upon me that day and in the days to come.

"The man who injured you did not stop?"

"No, Excellency."

"Come with me," she motioned.

"Mother Semple," she addressed my mother as we walked towards the door, "your daughter is in no trouble but we have business with the one that injured her. Hold her evening meal for her. I will return her before nightfall." My parents nodded. They were still in some shock after the healing of my hip.

As soon as we were out of my father's house, the Governor raised her scepter. A portal opened and we found ourselves in front of an impressive house of a mortal. Elaine's daily angelic escort preceded her; the smaller one, not the one used at ceremonial events. This escort was still a daunting sight. I could see a stable at the rear of the house. This man chose to transport himself by horse instead of machine; it was considered more elegant by some.

"Simon Wooster, come out here," Elaine said in a loud firm voice. A large well dressed man emerged almost immediately from the house along with what must have been most of his family. Some still had napkins tucked in their shirts. They had been interrupted while eating. I knew that this was not the man who had been riding the horse that had broken my hip. He was too old and too heavy.

"Your son, Adrian," the Governor demanded. She did not raise her voice.

"Excellency, I am so sorry, he is not at home," the man replied.

"I know, send for him," she responded.

There was a busy exchange of conversation among the family Wooster. There seemed to be some confusion as to where the son and heir was. Finally, two boys were dispatched in two different directions to find him.

"You would do well, Simon Wooster, to know where your son is and what he is doing," the Governor said.

"Yes, Excellency," Mr. Wooster responded, bowing. He was quite frightened. I was frightened for him. Somehow inside I was frightened just because everyone else seemed to be. Elaine looked into my eyes and I was suddenly totally at peace.

The young man Adrian came riding up with one of the boys on behind him. I recognized the animal. He ran over and knelt before the Governor.

"You injured this girl and did not stop." she said.

"I did not know," he started to lie, "I, … I am sorry, Excellency," his voice quivered. He knew better than to lie to an Immortal. They always knew. I had always thought that my mother was like them in this way.

"You will take the animal away from him," Elaine said, "and you will restrict his activities to the homestead for three months."

The boy looked up shocked. His father pushed his head down again.

"Yes, Excellency, it will not happen again." His fear seemed to be rising.

"This is a turning point, Simon," the Governor said.

"If I have to deal with him or you again, the punishment will be severe. Do you understand?" This time she did raise her voice slightly.

"Yes, Excellency, yes, yes, quite."

"Now, young man, you apologize to young Anna here. I have restored her hip which your mount shattered," Elaine said.

Adrian Wooster apologized profusely to me and I, of course, forgave him.

Elaine raised her scepter again, a portal opened and we stepped through and in an instant we were back at my father's house. I wondered what would happen if young Adrian did not improve. I knew that such sins as murder were punished with death right on the spot but I was not familiar with lesser infractions. It was later that I marveled at the way the Immortals traveled and were able to take us with them when they wanted to by opening a portal.

"Your daughter, Mother Semple," Elaine said. My entire family had gathered on the porch to wait.

"Thank you, Excellency," my mother said. She did not seem to be afraid.

"And you, young Anna, I will be back to take you some places," the Governor said. She smiled, raised her scepter slightly and she was gone. She and her angels did not need a portal.

I wondered where she was going to take me. I was excited. My family wanted to hear every detail of what had happened. I asked my father what he thought would happen if Adrian Wooster committed another infraction. Father said that he would probably be removed from his family and put under direct supervision if it was a minor offense, worse if it was not. I was afraid for him. He did not seem very sincere in his apology to me.

04.22.103 C.R. Every time I am caught writing in this dairy my family teases me. "What could you think or do that could be important enough to write down?" Mother would say. My brothers and sisters would always tell. "Anna is writing in her dairy," they would say. I keep on writing. Somehow I feel that it might be important some day. Father never seems to mind. I have written down Father's account of his grandmother's memory of the Glorious Return.

My great grandmother said that things had been very hard for all of mankind for a long time. Most people did not believe in the Glorious Return but my great grandmother at least hoped for it. All around there were wars. Some nations were stronger than others. When the stronger nation won, they would treat the losers terribly. Then when they managed to retaliate, they would be even more horrible to the defeated ones. America was the strongest and tried to do the right thing and keep the peace but eventually even it lost the ability to do so. There did not seem to be much love in the world. It was not peaceful like it is now under The Reign. Even though my great grandmother hoped for the return, she did not truly know God. That is why my family are still mortals. When it happened, those who truly knew God were changed. The rest of us lived on for our lifetimes and left children behind. Great grandmother said that she never really gave her heart to God because her husband would not have liked it. After the Return she wished that she had followed her heart and not her husband. But then it was too late. Anyway, things were pretty bad on the earth in those days. There had been wars and large poisonous dust clouds would hang over large parts of the earth. Food was hard to grow and many people would steal or kill to eat. It looked like mankind would soon wipe itself from the face of the earth.

Then early one morning, they say it was about 4 o'clock, it happened. Everywhere a trumpet sound was heard. Then an enormous releasing angelic shout. The graves of many of the dead opened and their bodies received life and jumped up into the sky. Then those who truly knew God were transformed. They got Immortal bodies and joined the rest in the sky over the earth. Thousands upon thousands of Angels were seen with the Emperor as he descended. The light from His face was so bright that no one could look upon it, brighter than the sun when the dust clouds did not cover the earth. Then and there He established his rule over the earth. He appointed sub-rulers everywhere, like Elaine over Buckhead and Prince Henry Sawyer over the entire Atlanta Metropolis. The angels quickly cleaned up all the mess that the wars and poisons had made and people were able to raise food again. Life for mortals became peaceful. We did not really know what it was like for the Immortals. They would come and go. We knew that they could go anywhere they wanted on the earth, but they went other places also. Sometimes they were overheard talking about their travels among themselves.

05.07.103 C.R. About three weeks after the incident with my hip the Governor Elaine returned to take me on a trip. I had finished my schooling and was helping mother around the house. I was faintly aware that I should by now have had a suitor, but none was forthcoming. Father's kindness sustained me. The Governor's arrival was, as usual, instantaneous and there was no time to prepare to leave.

"Mother Semple, I have come to take your daughter Anna on a short tour," Elaine said. "I will provide all her needs. We will be gone for several weeks. Please do not worry about anything regarding her." My mother nodded and we were gone. This time I was determined to note how I felt and what happened while we were being transported. I did not feel or see a thing or even remember anything during the transport. Suddenly, we were just there.

We arrived at the Dais of his Excellency Henry Sawyer, Metropolitan of Atlanta. The Dais was on top of a hill overlooking the Metroplex. It was a smooth grassy place with several white chairs and settees arranged in a semicircle overlooking the city. I had heard it said that the hill was actually the product of a terrible bomb used during one of the last wars before the Return of the Emperor, but now it was a most pleasant place. Metropolitan Sawyer is a large and happy Immortal. He sat in the center seat of the semicircle. On either side of him were three sub-rulers of which my Governor Elaine was one. One seat was empty, just to the left of the Metropolitan. This was reserved for the Emperor Himself. I wondered if he ever came here. I was awestruck and frightened at the same time. Elaine brought me forward to meet the Metropolitan.

"Henry, this is the young mortal I was telling you about," she said. I knelt before him. He helped me up.

"Hello, young lady," he said with a smile in his voice. "So you're the one that Elaine has been so impressed with." I did not know that she had been impressed with me.

"If you say so, my Lord."

"Yes, indeed, I do say so; a 'selfless, sweet girl,' she says. A mortal that we might want to have around. How would you like to be attached to my court, young lady?"

"Oh, yes, . . . my Lord, a, a great honor," I managed to reply.

"Then you are. We will keep you with us. Your parents will be informed." He nodded to an angel that was nearby. I was so rattled I could not remember if the angel had been there when I was introduced or not. But the angel was gone immediately, presumably to tell my folks. I thought that mother might be upset.

"Don't worry, girl," the Metropolitan said, " your parents will be at peace with this." I was shown to one of several small gatherings to the rear of the Dais by Elaine and she told one of the mortal women to take care of me. I was given a room of my own in a building there and shown where we were to eat. I wondered what was the purpose of my being here. Was I to perform some particular function? The other mortals were quite nice and I knew that I would like it there. I was attached to the court of the Immortal Metropolitan of Atlanta.

[N.D.] After a few days when no particular duties were assigned to me and I had not seen Elaine – she had gone through a portal to one of those places that Immortals go to from time to time I asked an older girl, Sheila Jones, what we were to do.

"You will be told when you're needed," she said. "It will not be too hard and there is nothing to be afraid of, they just seem to want us, to want us . . . , to well, be around, that's all. We do learn a lot about them." That was enough for me for the time being. In a few more days Elaine returned and sent for me.

They were all seated on the Dais and Elaine motioned for me to sit on the grass beside her. The Immortal on the other side seemed nice although a bit older, if that has any meaning for them. They seemed to be waiting for someone. In a few minutes angels started arriving. I say arriving. They would just suddenly appear a few hundred yards in front of the Dais; then they would move closer and form ranks around the Dais. One particular angel seemed to be in charge. I had seen angels before and I was not afraid of them although these were quite impressive. They look a lot like people, mortals or Immortals, but they were very white and bright and there was something hazy behind their backs although they do not actually have wings with feathers like the birds have. They were always kindly in appearance and moved with a certainty about themselves. After a few minutes several hundred had arrived. The Immortals on the Dais stood, I started to get frightened. Who was it? What would happen? Then suddenly a small dark woman appeared. The Immortals nodded. I got down on my knees.

"Henry, how good to see you," the new arrival said.

"Janice, and you, welcome, welcome to your city," Henry Sawyer said. He gave her his seat and another one was brought for him. There was still the empty seat beside them.

The new Prince had a longer scepter than Metropolitan Sawyer. They both had small crowns of golden olive leaves around their heads. I soon learned that our visitor was the Prince Janice Holland, Governor of the East Coast of which Atlanta was only a part. She was the

Over-Lord. I later learned that all governors had a Metropolitan over them and that all Metropolitans had an Over-Lord. That over the many Over-Lord's there were two Viceroys, one in the East and one in the West, and then the Emperor Himself. Among themselves the Immortals all just seemed like old friends, very casual and always happy. Why not? There was nothing that could threaten them.

As they visited and talked about their former lives as mortals I sat spellbound. What must it have been like? Some of them had been killed in the wars. Some of them were killed for their faith in those dark days before the Return of the Emperor.

In a little while an angel appeared at the Dais and spoke quietly to the Metropolitan. A mortal had committed some offence and another Immortal was bringing him for judgment. They appeared and the man was very frightened.

"He has killed his neighbor," the Immortal said. The Metropolitan Sawyer looked at his Over-Lord. She nodded back for him to handle it. He picked up his scepter from the little table beside his chair.

"You have killed your neighbor out of greed and hatred," he said. The man cringed. The Metropolitan pointed his scepter at the man. A look of terror crossed his face.

"That field should have been mine," the man said.

"But it was not. Why did you kill him?"

"As I said, er, Excellency, it should have been mine."

"How do you feel about killing him?" the Metropolitan asked.

"Well, I . . ."

"Never mind," the Metropolitan said. "You are guilty." All of the color left the man's face.

"A life for a life," the Metropolitan said. And the man fell over dead. Another wave of the scepter and two angels whisked the body away.

"Back to his family for burial," Elaine whispered to me. I had never seen such a thing. I thought everyone was too afraid of judgment to disobey the Ten Laws. They returned to their conversations as if nothing had happened. Well, I thought, that was what they are here for. They judge and keep the peace. I was glad they were here; it gave life the secure feeling that we mortals had become accustomed to over the generations. The mortals at court talked a lot about this judgment over the next several days.

11.12.103 C.R. Elaine had said that I might be interested in reading some of the records of the times when she herself was a mortal. I went to the Metropolitan's library and looked for something interesting. I had learned in school about the general time line back then. I knew that the main difference for them as mortals was the uncertainty; the terrible uncertainty in which they lived not knowing what new power would emerge and overrun the world or what disasters awaited them. Yet those who loved the Emperor had the Helper within their own bodies. But we lived in total peace during the Great Reign.

I looked very hard but could not find any record of Elaine's mortal life. When I asked her about this, she told me that I would do well to concentrate on some of the other Immortals. I wondered what the Metropolitan Henry Sawyer had done to win his reward. And the governor Janice of the East Coast. What had she done? I would be gone for whole days studying these ancient records which were printed on leaves of paper bound into binders in the library near the Metropolitan's residence. I was a ward of Elaine and I had not been assigned any other duties and she seemed content for me to do this. If I had been at home with my own dear mother and father, they would have soon put a stop to it so that I could help around our small garden and with my younger brothers and sisters. I wondered who had written the pages that I was reading. Surely an

Immortal would not have done this menial task. They already knew everything. And they could scarcely have written them while they were still mortal during those hard and cruel times. I finally concluded that they had been written by some mortals during the reign of the Emperor, people like myself. But these writings seemed disorganized and incomplete.

I looked long and hard for references to our Metropolitan. Then I found him. When I did, I sat in shocked silence for a long time. Henry Sawyer had been the primary inquisitor for the people who had abused the believers in the Emperor. As a matter of fact, he had personally done much harm and inflicted great pain on many of them. After many had died under his hand, he seemed to have changed. He started seeking out their friends and they would try to hide because they knew who he was. Nevertheless, he found a few of them and they shared their beliefs in the Emperor with him. To their surprise Henry Sawyer did not torture them. He wanted to know more. One night after a long discussion with one of them Henry Sawyer converted. He tried to keep it a secret from his old companions and succeeded for a long time, about 2 years. Then he could hide no longer. He started releasing prisoners and helping them to escape to the Southwest which had become a haven for these people. The believers had fortified themselves in places like this. But eventually Henry was caught and treated terribly. He managed to escape with the help of some of his own hidden secret converts. He did this again and again. Each time he was caught, he was tortured terribly. He would manage to escape and return for more people. Each time he was tortured he would affirm his belief in this wonderful absent Emperor. He was finally hung up with wires through his hands and died for his faith in this very area. For this he was made Metropolitan of Atlanta upon the Emperor's return and Elaine was one of his local governors. How could they now be such friends? I was a little confused by these Immortals.

03.19.104 C.R.   I started looking for records about Governor Janice. Her full title was Over Lord of the East Coast Of The Americas. Over her was the Viceroy Of The Western Hemisphere. Over him was the Emperor.   I wondered what he was like? They often went to Jerusalem to attend the Emperor's court.   But mortals were never asked to accompany them.

03.21.104 C.R.   It was very difficult to find references to the immortal Janice Holland. I finally found some references to what I believed to be her in a list of the hopelessly insane. There was nothing more.

05.23.104 C.R. The more I read, the more I wanted to compile the most inspiring parts into well organized books. I decided that I wanted to make this my life's work. I told Elaine and she seemed very happy. She said that she would do everything she could to help me. I had found a calling.   There had to be a testimony to those days for mortals of my generation and beyond to read.   As time went on, I had a growing desire to ask to interview Janice Holland but I was afraid to ask. One day a conversation with Elaine made it possible. I was walking a favorite walking trail near the Metropolitan's residence when Elaine appeared just ahead. This time I was startled even though I was used to such things.
"I'm sorry child," Elaine said.
She hurried to me and hugged me. I always love being hugged by an Immortal. They are so much like us only different in a way that I have vainly tried repeatedly to explain.
"How's our girl?" she asked with her arm still around me.

21

"Fine." I knew that I was smiling from ear to ear. She is so dear to me.

"Good! I am sorry that I have not seen you for so long. I have had to be away on matters of the Empire."

"And how is the Emperor?" I asked foolishly.

Elaine smiled. "The Emperor, my dear, is always fine, much, much more than fine."

I smiled back weakly, uncertainly.

"How is your research going?" she asked.

"Fine, fine but I need, er, I think I need some information that is not in those pages. Lots more information." I looked up into her eyes. Elaine is a full 8 inches taller than I am.

"Anna, that is wonderful. I, we, were so hoping that you would really throw yourself into this." I was glad that I was fulfilling their expectations.

"Elaine, I need more on the Over-Lord Janice."

"Yes, I image that you do. That is very special."

I waited. She seemed to read my thoughts.

"However, the only way to get that is from her own mouth," Elaine said. I shall tell her about your request and have you temporarily attached to her court." It was so easy and so sensible that I forgot to be nervous.

In a few days as I pouring over the old pages yet again, an angel about my size suddenly appeared. I jumped. They can be quite startling even though we know that they mean us no harm and that they were under the Immortals in rank.

"Mistress Anna," it said.

I nodded trying to keep my composure.

"Her Excellency, Janice Holland, bids you join her court. I am to deliver you," the angel said.

"Fine. And what is your name?" I asked. I was getting bolder being attached to a court.

"My name is Lucius."

"That's a good name for an angel," I said. He nodded.

For some reason this time I closed my eyes. I knew that the trip would be instantaneous but I did not want to watch. This time Elaine was not here to hold my hand. I was traveling alone with an angel. "OOOhhhhh! Ahh!" I opened my eyes. I found myself on another Dais, much larger than Henry Sawyer's, overlooking the ocean on one side and a very large city on the other.

"So, here is my little biographer."

I turned to see the Over-Lord approaching me. I knelt. She put one hand under my chin and pulled my face gently upward. Some more upward pressure bid me to rise. So I did. I towered over her in height. I had not remembered that she was so tiny.

"So, you want to write my story, child?"

"Yes, Excellency."

She glanced around at her court. They all smiled back.

"The story of an insane woman."

They all laughed. I knew that this would be interesting.

07.10.104 C.R.   Those who hated the absent Emperor in her area took a different approach than those who had lived farther to the South. After the bombings a group of people there had taken control and persecuted those loyal to the Emperor. Instead of beatings they had resorted to drug injections which some of them had learned from a group across the ocean. If you would not denounce the Emperor, you were declared insane and given these injections. At first you would merely feel disoriented. But if you did not denounce the Emperor, they would increase the dosage until you were in extreme mental and emotional distress and actually forgot most of what you knew. They called this "washing your brain." Eventually they would get you to say the words and sign a paper denying the Emperor. But to their surprise Janice would never deny him no matter what they did to her. She said that the Helper lived in her at a much deeper level than her mind or her emotions. Her mind and emotions were just as damaged as any other prisoners. Her behavior was indeed insane. She would know nothing and she would drool constantly. But she would not deny. When the Emperor returned, she had been lying on her bed with nothing but water and gruel for weeks. She knew nothing. The Emperor immediately restored her. She had been a teacher in a religious school for over 30 years before they captured her. It was called being a "Nun." She said that as soon as the Emperor drew her into the air, she was totally restored and the Emperor gave her a coronet for her head and her scepter and told her to deal with her tormentors and to rule for him. This she did.

11.22.111 C.R.   For many years now I have kept my study near the Metropolitan's court in a small building that they have provided for me there. I am absorbed in my work. It is known throughout this hemisphere what I am doing and perhaps even in the Eastern one as well. Lucius has never left me from that first time he came and took me to interview Janice. He watches over me day and night. At first I thought I would never get used to being watched continually, but I did. He rarely speaks and when he does it is very softly. He is a gentle creature unless I am threatened, then he grows larger and brighter. When I want to go anywhere, he will take me. If I ask him to take me somewhere and he does not comply, I know that it is forbidden. But, for the most part, we are allowed to go anywhere. I never remember the trip, only the instant before the departure and after the arrival. I quit closing my eyes as it does not make any difference. After Lucius had been with me for some time, it occurred to me to ask Elaine what he had done before the return of the Emperor. She told me that he had attended her personally; he was her personal guardian. But she had never seen him until all the angels became visible upon the return of the Emperor. Their times as mortals had certainly been different from ours.

01.22.112 C.R.   The very special day that I am going to tell you about, reader, began as any other day. It was sunny and a little cool. The earth was beautiful and I was awakened by Lucius who told me that once again Elaine wanted me to join her at the Dais. Lucius never sleeps. I wondered if there would be another visit from the Over-Lord   Janice. I dressed quickly and joined my Mistress, Elaine, at the Dais. I sat by her feet on the grass. Several of the other Immortals greeted me and I responded respectfully, aware of my special privileges as a mortal which Elaine has given me. Sure enough before long angels started appearing before the Dais. Elaine had told me that when Janice had come that there was one whole legion of angels that preceded her. Soon I was aware that at least twice as many had appeared. There were so many this time that they spread out after coming through the portal and formed a semi-circle in the air facing the Dais. They just kept coming and coming. I was getting more and more excited and a little frightened. After what must have been six legions had arrived, an enormous angel appeared. He nodded to the immortal princes and they nodded respectfully in return. I heard Elaine say softly, "Gabriel." He was larger in every way than the other angels and had an enormous head which sent forth a beautiful glow. I knew who he was but I had never seen him. He was magnificent. To my surprise the angels kept pouring through the portal. I asked myself, who could be greater than Gabriel? My breath left my chest. The Emperor!

I had been watching the Immortals out of the corner of my eye for some clues. Before I could catch my breath, I saw the Immortals on the Dais fall on their faces and throw their crowns and scepters on the ground in front of them. I was terror stricken. I fell on my face behind Elaine and grabbed her ankle with my left hand and held on for dear life. Suddenly the air was full of a sweet, sweet scent and I felt wonderfully light headed. I remember thinking briefly, good, maybe I will pass out and die right here on this spot of grass. I heard the immortals shout praises to the Emperor. Then I heard his voice. It sounded like a hundred gentle waterfalls. Instantly I was at peace. Elaine had pulled away from my grasp and I was left on my own. I don't know where I got the strength to look up but I lifted my head slightly to get a glimpse of him. I was surprised. Looking at his profile he seemed to be just a man. He was much smaller than the Metropolitan Henry Sawyer. He had medium long hair and a full beard that was not very long. He wore a simple white robe. He was not wearing a crown or coronet or carrying a scepter. He looked my way and before I could divert my eyes, we made eye contact. I felt like a lightning bolt had just passed through my brain but I was not injured and I knew it. I put my face back on the ground.

Everything grew silent and before long I was sure that I could hear footsteps in the grass coming my way. I hoped that it was Elaine but I could tell that it was not. He put his hand on my shoulder and applied some upward pressure so I sat up. I was filled with peace. I sat there on my heals and looked into his eyes. I was lost in them. I swam in his eyes for what seemed forever. I was completely absorbed. Later when I met the man I was to marry, I loved to look into his eyes and I was aware of him and of myself and my own body very strongly. Lost in the emperor's eyes I was only aware of Him. I was drowning in love. It was wonderful. Words fail me to explain it. I can not to this day describe total joy. But I experienced it then; the absence of every other feeling or emotion or thought except absolute joy, joy abounding and eternal. When I was in the state of love with the Emperor, everything else flew away. Somewhere I must have known that there was a world there. But it would wait, everything and everybody waited for Him.

After a while he smiled and took his hand off of my shoulder. I saw wounds in his hands. He smiled and walked back to the Dais. He sat in the chair to the Metropolitan's left which was always reserved for him. The crowns and scepters remained on the ground and no one seemed to care. These precious things which had been purchased by so much devotion in their mortal lives lay like trash. What an experience! I felt that I could live to a ripe old age on this experience alone, and indeed, I did.

[N.D.] Later I told Elaine how I felt when I looked into the Emperor's eyes. I must have looked very surprised because she said. "Yes, yes, dear Anna. We feel the same way." I could not respond; they were Immortals and these Immortals were princes as well. There were some who weren't actually princes.

"You see, Anna," Elaine continued. "The Emperor is God. We are Immortal by his power only. Someday, who knows, maybe you will be Immortal too. But the Emperor is God, God Himself." I did not understand it, but I accepted it.

[N.D.] One day about three months after I saw the Emperor, Elaine signaled Lucius to bring me to her house.

"Anna, dear, come, come to me," she motioned.

I went and sat next to her.

"I have something for you, dear."

"Yes," I answered.

She motioned and a mortal man entered the room.

"Daniel, this is our Anna," Elaine said.

This man was gorgeous. He was tall and blond with light gray eyes. As soon as I looked into them, I was his. We stared at each other for a long time. I hoped desperately that he was half as attracted to me as I was to him.

My Governor silently left the room at some point, I was unaware.

Daniel and I exchanged our life stories. We talked for hours, night came and day broke again. Daniel lived nearby in Elaine's own principality. He came to see me often and we would walk in the garden behind the Dais. He told me that he had loved me from the first day. After about three months we asked Elaine for permission to marry. She gave it cheerfully.

07.18.114 C.R. Our wedding was a very public affair. It seems that there is something about weddings that interests the Immortals. Soon after we talked to Elaine, it set off a flurry of activity in the Metropolitan's court. We were honored to have the attention, but we were very surprised. My original intention in talking to Elaine about it was to find out if it would be acceptable to her. After that, we intended to go to my parents for their blessing. I had taken Daniel to eat at my parent's house and they were obviously very happy about him. By now they had abandoned any hope of my marrying. After I received Elaine's blessing, we did go to my parents and they gave us their enthusiastic support. But Elaine quickly informed me that the Metropolitan himself wanted to perform the ceremony at the Dais. We were overcome. We set a date barely two months away and my mother began inviting everyone. Daniel's parents were also subjects of the Over-Lord Janice and they came down with several uncles and aunts and many cousins. It fell to my parents and uncles and aunts and cousins to put them up. Everyone was assigned to someone and the time flew by until suddenly it was our wedding day. We all went to the Dais and I waited in my small office with my bridesmaids to be called. When it was time, Elaine came for me.

"You may be somewhat surprised, little one," Elaine said. She often called me by that name when she wanted to express her affection for me although by now we both appeared to be about the same age. I thought that perhaps as I was about to be a married woman, she would find another term for me. As we proceeded to the Dais, I found that there were literally thousands of mortals there and many more Immortals than I had ever seen in one place and quite a large contingent of angels on the outer area around the Dais. These Immortals love weddings. I did not know at the time that the Emperor had performed his first miracle at a wedding and that the relationship between the Emperor and the Immortals was likened in the ancient books to a marriage relationship. In their previous mortal state the entire company of those referred to as "believers" in the world had been known as the bride of the Emperor. I intended to look into this further in my studies after my wedding trip. The ceremony was beautiful. Mother had coordinated all of the details with Lucius. It had taken her a few days to get over her apprehension of dealing directly with an angel on this matter, but once she was accustomed to it, she really liked it. No one knew of any other mortal, even mortal administrators who had been personally assigned an angel. The Metropolitan wished us every happiness and Lucius transported us to a beautiful tropical island for a 10 day wedding trip. My father and uncles had given us some gold to pay for the lodging and food but we were given far more by our hosts than we could have ever paid for.

[N.D.]   After we returned from our trip, the Metropolitan gave us a residence not far from the Dais. The house is very nice but not too large. My husband registered to grow certain food crops on the land since there is considerable land that goes with the house. He feels that this is the way that he can contribute to the overall good of our society and he will receive compensation for his crops. I had never asked for more than my keep in my work so other compensations had never been discussed. I believe that Daniel is doing the right thing. I travel when necessary with Lucius and I have moved all of the study materials from my little study near the Dais to a new study set up in our home. Daniel is a fine husband and in the third year of our marriage I gave birth to the next great love of my life, our son Mark.

[N.D.]   After Mark was weaned, I set out to establish an overall plan for my writing. I decided on three primary categories. The first part which I am calling the First Testament is an organization and commentary on the first section of the ancient writings revered by the Immortals. It concerns the creation of the earth and the ancient Empire of the people of God. It covers in summary about 4,000 years. The Second Testament is all about the Emperor including when he came to earth as a humble man and when he died his heroic death and returned from the dead. This is the shortest work although the most important and covers only about 33 years. The Third Testament is about the lives of the Immortals when they were mortal after the Emperor went back to His Father. That is the most difficult part for me because it has not been previously written in a clear form; so I have to do all of the research and organizing and writing myself. This part covers just over 2,000 years although the first and last 200 years seem to be the more important eras. Even Daniel does not attempt to enter into my writing. It seems that it is my task alone. Not too many mortals take much of an interest in what I am doing but the Metropolitan and his court seem to think it is important. I wonder sometimes if there are others like me in other courts of the Empire that are doing the same kind of work, but I have not found anyone so far in my travels.

01.22.115 C.R. Daniel is allowed to accompany me on my travels and if it is the right season, he will come with me. He never puts himself forward and I must admit that I do not pay him the attention that he deserves. When Mark was very young, I did not travel as much as I do now. We seldom take him with us as there is always a mortal child caregiver assigned to us. I generally take at least one trip a month to the library attached to some court. At first Elaine would arrange these trips but now I just tell Lucius and he takes care of everything. We are always welcomed cordially by a mortal aide. This is, I suppose, because of Lucius. If I need an audience with the Immortal Prince of the area, Lucius arranges that as well. Elaine is always interested in my progress when I return. Once in a while I encounter her at some other court and we are always glad to see each other. Aside from Daniel I think that she is my best friend; a strange thing for a mortal to have.

05.22.115 C.R. We live in a wonderful peace under the Emperor. My research has shown that there are many things that are not the same for us mortals compared to the pre-reign systems, the ones that our Immortals had when they were mortal. They had many nations with many different kinds of rulers and systems.

We use gold as our exchange all over the Empire. It is struck in coins with the symbol of the Emperor on it. It is not permitted to use his image or even his profile. These coins are struck by the Imperial Bank which is staffed by mortals under the oversight of the Imperial Controller who is an Immortal. Many of our needs are supplied by the Imperial Commissary which does not require gold. Like the bank it is staffed by mortals under the Immortal Imperial

Commissioner. Only private exchanges are negotiated with gold. This is permitted so long as it does not compete with the Commissary. The Commissary is funded by the Imperial Bank and the items that they dispense are without charge. Private transactions are not permitted to compete with the Commissary so that people will not be deprived or treated unfairly. All necessary food, clothing, housing and transportation are supplied by the Commissary on the basis of need; there is a continuous supply. Things like jewelry and fancy clothing and specialty foods and drink are sold on the gold basis. We get gold from our work with private mortal organizations or our work for Immortals who maintain homes in this world. Our system is not as complicated as the pre-reign system was. They had many different banks and systems which, near the end, were tied together by an extensive electronic system. There are no electronic communications like there were before the Reign. This has been dictated by the Viceroys as, in the end, it seemed to do more harm than good.

We have published newspapers and books. Those under Imperial license are free. There are also private ones. Writings of rebellion against the Emperor are not permitted. Land travel is by train. There are boats for the sea. They are powered by steam and burn natural fuels to propel them. For lighting we burn oil lamps. Most people live and work locally. There are no airplanes just as there are no electronic communications. As a result, the two hemispheres are somewhat isolated. Mortals can be transported by angels. This does not happen very often. I am the only mortal with a personal angel to assist me. That is because Elaine has provided Lucius to me. Elaine has more authority than any other sub-ruler that I have ever met. This seems strange but I do not question it.

Abuse of chemical substances is not permitted. War is unknown. The killing of unborn children is not permitted. People can marry by obtaining a license from the local civil administrator. If they conceive outside of marriage, they must then marry. Divorce is permitted on the authority of the civil administrators. Multiple spouses are not permitted. Any couple that conceives a child is responsible for their care; however, if one or both parents die, the children are placed with foster parents. There are many who love to do this.

There are no prisons. Wrong doers are either executed at judgment or put under probation with attending angels until the local ruler deems it appropriate to free them. There is always an abundance of angels. They seem to know when offenses are committed and sometimes an Immortal investigator will be contacted who will take offenders to a ruler judge. Otherwise, the angels take them directly. Because of the knowledge of the Immortals and the angels the facts of a crime are never in doubt.

Many Immortals who are not princes enjoy the natural areas of the earth. Some maintain residences there, but mortals who voluntarily work as servants must be paid in Imperial gold coin and are always treated with respect and fairness. There are no weather related or other natural disasters because the Emperor controls these things and does not allow them. Any Immortal can travel to be with the Emperor in places that we can not go. They do this often. They always return even happier than they were when they departed.

There are no medical care facilities. There is very little sickness among us. Any Immortal can dispense healing to us and we live healthily. We die peacefully in simple old age. We usually live about 70 to 90 years.

Education is simple and provided by the Imperial Education Trust. It is administered by mortal administrators under the Immortal Imperial Principal. The administrators and the teachers are provided with all the necessities of living. For private tutoring they are paid with Imperial coin. Everyone is taught to read and write and to make necessary calculations. Those who want to serve the Emperor in more advanced ways, like teaching or administration, can pursue further study.

Daniel gives the food he raises to the local food administrator. All of our needs are provided by the Emperor through Elaine. Our lives are good and we are thankful.

03.16.116 C.R.   The Viceroy of the Eastern half of the World is John the Beloved. His court is located on Patmos Island which is fairly close to the capital. This is because John spent some years on that island just before his death and because the Viceroy never wants to be far from the Emperor even if he can travel instantaneously to His side. No mortal, including myself, can approach the Imperial Court in Jerusalem without an invitation. However, I can visit a Viceroy's court if I have a suitable reason. I have been considering for years what a suitable reason might be for visiting the Viceroy's court and his substantial library. I now believe that I have collected sufficient reasons. Of course, there is always the Western Viceroy's court which is closer to where I live but it is far from the capital and I suspect, rightly or wrongly, that there are fewer important answers to be found there. Additionally, John the Beloved knew the Emperor when he came as a man and Luis Cepata did not. Before I asked Lucius to arrange the trip, I talked to Daniel to make sure that he could accompany me. Mark is twelve now, but I believe that we shall leave him at the residence with the servants. Lucius disappeared to get permission and returned in about an hour to say that the answer would be forthcoming in a few days. I asked him if I had overstepped my privilege. He said that I had not.

As we were promised, permission came in a few days but we were instructed not to come for another week. I busied myself with more relevant research in case Elaine or any Immortal, even the Viceroy, should question my reason for the visit.

[N.D.] This morning Elaine came to tell me that she would accompany us to Patmos Island. I was a little taken back but perhaps I had begun to think too highly of myself and my position. I was polite and accepting while she was here but after she departed, I was concerned about my attitude. I asked to see her again at her convenience. She came back to me and I told her that I was sorry. She said that I had done nothing to be sorry about. I hugged her before she left. We arrived at Patmos Island just behind Elaine's full ceremonial escort which now seemed large to me for an under Prince. I have seen quite a lot in the past few years. We would have some time at the Dais before I could begin my research.

[N.D.] The angelic canopy over Patmos Island is magnificent. It is gigantic and beautiful. It is second only to the one over Jerusalem and equal to the one over the Western Viceroy's court in Montevideo. There are always angels visible over the city; the numbers vary but there are always plenty in view. They are very bright and they will produce magnificent choral chords for about a half an hour, and then they will be silent and change their formations in a beautiful coordinated manner. Their formations center on the Dais which is very large. The Viceroy's seat is in the middle of the top tier with three settee's on each side which seat two under governor's each. There are seven settee's on the middle tier and nine on the lower tier. I understand that of all the Dais' in the world only the two Viceroys have a multi-tiered Dais. There is no Dais in Jerusalem as the Emperor holds court in the reconstructed Palace next to the Temple. The construction of the Dais and the surrounding buildings including the Viceroy's massive residence took more space than the small island had to give. So, more

Island was constructed to accommodate all of the structures and the surrounding parks. My research tells me that many mortals volunteered to help in the construction throughout the hemisphere but that the angels were responsible for much of the heavier work.

Elaine was warmly welcomed by the Viceroy himself. She introduced me to the Viceroy. Physically he is much like the Emperor in size and shape and the way he grooms his hair and beard. I am told that they do not actually have to groom themselves; their hair and beards are as they will them to be. The Viceroy is somewhat darker than the Emperor and he wears a coronet on his head and carries a scepter just as the rulers under him do. Only the Emperor does without these accessories. John's coronet is much like the others but his scepter, although no larger that my Metropolitan's or Janice's, is different. It is plainer and has only a small cross on the tip.

John is certainly worthy of the title, "Beloved." Love seems to flow from his person. Having had the honor of meeting the Emperor I can honestly say that John the Beloved stands only under the Emperor in the love and power that radiates from him. Everyone at his court seems to pick up on this radiating love and projects it to everyone around. We were positively drunk in their presence. My dear husband was even more overwhelmed than I. He had never met the Emperor and he has a very dear and sensitive nature. I commented to Elaine about this afterward in our private rooms. Our rooms were next to Elaine's.

"You do sense the love which flows from the Viceroy just as we do?" I asked.

"Yes, it is very strong. He is the apostle of love."

"Daniel is quite overwhelmed," I said. Daniel had retired early.

"Good. He needed this," Elaine replied. "You know Anna, the reason that the Viceroy gives so much love is because he is constantly going to the Emperor."

"Explain, please."

"He goes to the capital and visits and embraces the Emperor every chance he gets. He has many duties here so he can not stay for long with the Emperor, but he makes many, many short trips. He says that he must do this."

"So all this love does not originate with the Viceroy?" I asked.

"Darling, all love originates with the Emperor. John just practices constant exposure to the source," Elaine said.

It took me a while to absorb this but I could understand it because I had been lost in the Emperor's eyes for a few moments myself once years ago. I talked about it with Daniel.

[N.D.] The Viceroy's library is extensive and I have spent many weeks sifting through much of it. I have five mortal aides for the work and even Lucius has helped. Two questions have begun to plague me. The first question is, why did the Emperor and the Immortals set up his rule over us mortals on the earth in the first place? They seem to enjoy being together "away" from the world. I have become convinced that it is not because they simply love to be Lords over us. Many times they seem almost burdened with the task. Perhaps it is because they know what we would do to each other without them and it is an act of love towards us. This may be partially true, but I am convinced that it is not the entire answer. The second question is, will it all end and, if so, when and how? For some reason I believe that the Imperial Reign will come to an end, not because any mortal can defeat the Emperor but because someday he would simply go "away" and the Immortals will go with Him. But the why or when I do not know. I will continue searching. I do not know at this time if these answers, for they must exist, will be appropriate to publish at least in my lifetime. I do keep a private journal and I will leave these answers or all that I can find about them to Mark. Sooner or later, they must be answered.

02.12.157 C.R.   Today I was officially recognized as mortal Compiler Of Histories. Elaine nominated me to Viceroy Cepata and our Metropolitan Henry and Over-Lord Janice endorsed it. I am so honored and Daniel is so happy for me. The Viceroy even indicated that the Emperor is pleased with my work. The award, in the form of a medal on a red ribbon was placed around my neck by Elaine at the Over-Lord's Dais. Lucius took us to the Dais and returned us to our residence afterwards.

03.22.158 C.R.   I lost Daniel last week. He was seventy-three years of age. He passed quietly and Elaine was by my side. I have not made any entries in my journals since then until now. It hit me very hard. We were very close and he was always such a dear husband. I am almost as old as Daniel so I have decided to begin training Mark to do my work.

"True, he is her son, her only child. But he does not act like her," the Metropolitan said.

"He cried for days at her death," Elaine said. "I had to assure him continually that there was great hope for her resurrection. He has her mind and her heart, Henry. As a child his tenderness was most apparent. You yourself noticed that."

"Now, however," Henry Sawyer continued, "he has been reminding me more of the rebellious masses that we are put here to contain."

"I understand, Henry," Elaine continued. "But that is just his age. He will grow out of it."

"And, and my dear Elaine," Sawyer continued, "he wants to visit beyond the veil, in what they call 'away' with the Emperor or the 'next-door-place.' Now, Elaine, you know that he can not do that. It is a physical impossibility. His mortal body would perish if he were even able to attempt it."

"I have told him that, Henry, and he will not ask again. But isn't that very desire a good thing in itself. He wants to be more than he now is."

"Yes, and didn't we all?" the Metropolitan responded in a softer tone. "None of us could have endured unless we had desired the reward. But he will have to wait for his own transformation, if the Emperor will grant it. I am only concerned that he has become so familiar with being with us that he does not have his mother's gratitude for it all."

"Yet, Henry," Elaine said, "yet you do acknowledge that the Emperor has given me the authority to approve Anna's successors?"

"Yes, Elaine, you know that I do. And we all here also do not forget," he waved his arm to include all the *immortals seated at the Dais,* "*that even though the mortals do not know it, you are the Imperial Legate here and that your particular mission here has a special significance. However, please bear in mind that once the succession is started, the mortals will see the family of Anna, and indeed Anna herself, as being much more important than the work of Anna alone. Dynasties carry a lot of weight with people.*"

"*But is this not our purpose?*"

"*Yes, yes it is. But we must be sure of the boy. There are other choices. Anna's younger sister or one of her nieces or nephews. As a personal favor to me, Elaine, deal with the boy, take off the kid gloves.*"

"*Very well, Henry, my dear brother, I will be firmer.*"

2 * MARK

159 – 214 C.R.

03.19.159 C.R. My name is Mark. I am the son of Anna, the compiler of histories. It is the year 163 of the Glorious Reign. My mother has been gone four years now. For the first year I grieved much. Our blessed Immortal Elaine comforted me but there was only so much that she could do. To tell the truth I had not expected my mother to die. I knew that we were mortals and Elaine and her kind were immortal. I have read my mother's histories about the immortals before the reign so I understood with my mind how things were. But in my heart I could not accept the truth. My mother was the most favored of all mortals and yet she was not spared the ignominy of death. In my heart I was sad and angry at the same time. But I did not show my anger. I have even tried to quiz Lucius about some things. He is a gentle being but would usually refuse to answer. One day I worked up the courage to tell Lucius to transport me to Elaine which he did. Lucius is an angel and he had always done mother's bidding.

I asked Elaine about some things which are important to me.

"Why are you Immortal and I am mortal?"

"Mark, you know the history. I embraced the Emperor before he was visible."

"I understand the time line, Elaine. But why has mankind been divided by it. You were born. I was born. But, just because you were born earlier, you are Immortal and I am not. Is the Emperor unfair?"

"Mark, you delve into things that are too big for you. You must wait for your answers."

"I'll bet that when you go outside this world that you find out answers that you will not tell us."

"If that is true," Elaine paused, "it is for your own good and I am not obliged to tell you. The Emperor owes no one favor. He never has. I was honored to be chosen in my day. You should be in yours. Think, think of how it was with your mother when she first came to us. You have been with us all along. You forget yourself, Mark."

I felt that my response would be crucial.

"Yes, Elaine, I, I am grateful. And I will do my best to act like it."

05.12.159 C.R. Today Elaine took me to another area of the Metropolitan's realm while she inspected the water cleansing areas there. It is always good to travel with Elaine. We are about the same height and at this time we appear to be the same age. Sometimes when I travel with her, I am mistaken for an Immortal myself. On the last trip a man of about my age bowed his head to me. I signaled with a wave of my hand. At first he looked perplexed and then a look of recognition came to his face as he realized that I was as mortal as he. Then the look of recognition changed to a look of spite as if I had intentionally misled him. I am used to traveling with Elaine. I had done so since I was a very small boy. I did not call her "mistress" or "governor." This she had always allowed, but I did not want her to see me receiving any deference from another mortal. I knew that she would not be pleased. She finished her inspection in this place. It was a beautiful place of running streams and wooded lands. The people that lived there grew food for us like my father had done. When she was ready to depart, she looked in my direction. I ran to her side and was sure to smile. She raised her scepter, a portal opened and we were back by the Dais of the Metropolitan.

"Mark, go back to your house and wait until I send for you," she said.

I was a little surprised but I did as she commanded. I told myself that she was very busy. A few days went by and I was not summoned. Then more days, then weeks, then a month, then several months. By this time I was consumed with worry. I had been set aside by Elaine. Out of favor. She was aware of my jealousy of the Immortals. What was I to do?

10.12.159 C.R.   It has been many months now. Several times I have started to walk to the Dais to at least look in on Elaine and the others there. But I have suppressed the urge. I do not even know if Elaine is still in the area. She may have been called to Jerusalem or some other place. I have asked, then ordered Lucius to take me to Elaine several times, but he does not respond. I have busied myself with mother's writings and I have a great deal of knowledge now about the pre-reign era. Some who are now Immortals are scarcely better than we are. It is just that they were born before the Reign began. I am not sure that this is fair, but there is nothing that I can do about it. One of the primary advantages that we have is the absence of the evil prince. Since the return of the Emperor, the evil prince has been bound along with all of his angels and taken to some secret prison. The importance of this to us now is that any evil that we mortals commit is strictly from our own nature. That is why it is punished so quickly by the Immortals who rule and judge us.

It has now been just over two years since I have seen Elaine. Many of my fellow mortals no longer come to me for insight into mother's writings so I have much time on my hands. For some reason Lucius remains with me, but we seldom communicate. He stays at my house and is always near when I go out. I hear from some of my close friends that the local mortal assembly is split as to whether I am still the chosen one. Some, the majority, say that since I have not been invited to the Dais for over two years that I am not my mother's heir and that I should find ordinary employment. I have even been offered a few positions by several friends of my family. Then others argue that no one else has been appointed in my place. I am told that Elaine is seen regularly at the Dais now. But she does not send for me and I will not shame myself by going to her. Besides, she ordered me to wait until she summoned me. Also, the continued presence of Lucius at my side is another argument that I have not been set aside permanently. There is considerable confusion.

11.03.159 C.R. I think that I will travel. Father left me enough gold so that I can travel comfortably for a few years. Then I can come home and accept some kind offer of employment from one of our family friends. At least mother's position will continue to serve me well for many years to come. I have ordered Lucius to remain behind. I want to travel unrecognized.

11.11.159 C.R. I have been gone a week and I am already starting to learn a lot. Lucius has apparently obeyed my order and stayed behind. I have worked my way up the East Coast and nearing New York. I have been traveling on the free public train. Most of the time I have had a private compartment and I have made a few young friends so far on my journey. We go most places together; myself, and John and Martha and Cliff. We are all unmarried and about the same age.

11.29.159 C.R. Today we arrived in New York. What a great city! We will go adventuring. We have stayed up almost continuously for the better part of three days. Martha and John have found a public inn and say that they are going to sleep for a long time. Cliff and I still aren't tired. Night is approaching and we are going to another party. We have been exploring the streets of the city and have decided to walk to this party. It has been much advertised and a popular new poet, Adrian Harnecker, will be reciting some of his new verse.

11.30.159 C. R. We had quite a time last night. We have returned to the inn and I have had a few hours of sleep, but I awoke thinking about last night and I just have to put this in my diary. As Cliff and I walked down a dark and narrow street, it began to rain softly. We were not concerned as we enjoyed the rain and neither of us had ever been afraid of the dark. Suddenly five young men seemed to appear out of nowhere and demanded our gold. I looked at Cliff and we both knew that we would fight them before we would give up our gold. They all seemed much thinner and lighter then we are. Who do they think that are? Bandits in this day and age? Don't they know that they will be swiftly and strictly judged. We were squaring off to begin combat when one of the five spotted something over my shoulder. A look of abject fear crossed his face. I turned to see. It was Lucius. I had never seen Lucius look this big and bright and strong. The mere sight of him froze our opponents in their tracks. They started to flee. Lucius spoke firmly just once.

"Hold your places," he commanded.

They stopped and turned around. In a few seconds other angels arrived to take them to judgment. They looked very sad and scared. I thought, oh, well, they won't get much, probably just a strong warning. I remembered in my studies that before the reign they would have been taken to a jail. But now since everything is monitored by the angels and judged by the Immortals, such places are not needed. They are either warned or executed or linked to an angel for a probation period. A simple and effective system. As the other angels, four or them, prepared to leave, the last one looked my way and nodded. I looked around quickly for Lucius. Now he was gone. This recognition by the angel clear up here in New York made me wonder. I was still recognized by them. Perhaps I would someday be restored. Or perhaps it was just in deference to my mother. Anna had been much loved by them all, Immortal and angel alike.

We continued to the gathering and listened to the poetry of Adrian Harnecker. Adrian is a man of middle age, about twenty years older than myself. He is tall and bony and blonde. He sits on a stool and strums a small stringed instrument to accompany his poetry. His poetry is unusual. It does not always rhyme as I think it should. It is more the content of the poems that appeals to people of my age.

> It is not far but can't seem close,
> That place we long to be,
> To wait is hard.
> But choice is gone,
> For those who wish to see.
>
> I wish to see, I wish to hear,
> Those great eternal songs,
> Who will bring them all down here,
> Where soul and heart do long?
>
> Amazing Grace how sweet the sound,
> That saved a wretch like me.

I did not understand it all, but it still appealed to me.

12.06.159 C.R. A few days later I thought that while we were in the area I might as well visit the Dais of the East Coast Governor Janice. I don't know why I wanted to go, but I thought, why not? All mortals were allowed to the outermost marker around the Dais and I did not expect to be recognized. John and Cliff were not interested but Martha said that she would go. She had once been to the Dais of her Metropolitan to the South. We caught a public train to the area and walked up the hill. There were a fair amount of mortals visiting that day and we moved closer than I had intended. The Governor was there; I had seen her years ago at our Dais with my mother. Mother had talked to her; I was a young boy at the time. Janice was talking casually with her court as the Immortals so often do. Martha and I sat down on the grass to watch. Occasionally an angel would approach with one or another wrong doer. After about an hour and a half I was shifting my weight to stand and back away from the Dais. I presumed that Martha would follow my lead. It was then that I saw one of the young men who had attempted to take our gold. I told Martha who he was and we crept forward without rising to try to hear better.

"Killed?" Janice asked the angel.

The angel nodded, "Yes."

"Young man," the governor addressed the frightened youth, "do you know what you have done?"

The boy nodded. He looked so small and frightened.

Evidently this offender had done something worse just before he had attempted to rob us. I wondered why he had not been apprehended at that time.

Janice talked with the angel briefly. I began to wonder again how much the Immortals knew without the angels. Sometimes they seemed to know everything and sometimes they asked the angels for information. I had never figured it out.

"Young man, what is your name?" the governor asked.

"Bertrum," the boy muttered.

"Fortunately we were able to revive your intended victim," Janice said. "So you shall not die. However, you shall serve your victim until all of his strength returns. Then we shall decide what to do. Do not make the mistake of thinking that you can misbehave again or you will be very sorry. You will be tied to this angel. Do you understand?" She raised her voice with that last question.

Immediately an angel attached himself to the boy's arm. The boy seemed terrified. He nodded his head yes repeatedly. An angel was about to take him away when the governor spoke again.

"Do any of you mortals recognize this man?" she asked. She looked out among us. Many shook their heads no. I had no choice but to respond. To ignore an Immortal was a grave offense. I stood slowly. Martha looked up at me sympathetically.

"Yes, Excellency," I said clearly.

She looked at me.

"Young Mark?"

Martha was impressed.

"Yes, Excellency."

"What do you know?"

"Only that he tried to rob us of our gold, my friend and me, six nights ago, with three of his cohorts, Excellency."

"Multiple crimes. I am afraid young Bertrum, that you will have to serve with very limited vision. I will not take it all as you would then be useless to serve, but you will be limited in your ability to see and to act until and if I see that you have changed your ways."

The boy looked startled and held his hand in front of his face to see how much he could see.

"Good travels, young Mark," the governor said to me.

I nodded. She turned away and Bertrum and his escort passed through a portal to who knows where.

I took Martha's hand and we worked our way back and silently left the area of the Dais. So, I am still recognized by the princes of this world. Martha seemed in awe and held my hand for a very long time. She has nice hands and I enjoyed it. When we parted that evening, I did not want her to leave. But I did.. I would meet her in the morning and we would journey on.

[N.D.] When I arrived at Martha's inn the next morning, she was no where to be found. I enquired of the inn keeper vigilantly until I annoyed him.

"I told you, young man, the young woman you are seeking left here just before dawn and did not tell me or any of my staff where she was going. She took her pack with her and I do not expect her to return. Now leave me to my business."

"Yes, sir. Thank you very much."

Where had she gone? She had agreed to meet me. I thought that she liked me as much as I liked her. Perhaps the governor's familiarity had frightened her away. Perhaps she and John already had something going. This was confirmed to me when I could not find John either. I did locate Cliff and we traveled on together. He did not know where they were or even if they were together.

We decided to turn West. We began on the public train, but somewhere in the Dakotas we decided to rent a vehicle and see more of the countryside. There are a few old pre-reign electric models around; it had strong batteries which recharged from the sun. I began to be struck by the fact that travel was so easy because of the peace of the reign, the Pax Regnum. There was little danger and little want in the world. I was young and strong. Perhaps Elaine is right; I am not grateful enough.

[N.D.] After two days of hard driving we got lost. All around there was arid land and low mountains. It was hot. The car ran fine on the power of the sun. But Cliff and I were tired and hungry and rapidly running out of drink. We spotted a cloud of dust ahead of us and we chased it. This led us into a box canyon that could not be easily detected. The entrance was narrow and only visible from one direction. We followed the other vehicle in. We were soon surrounded. Everyone there was mortal. And they did not seem kind.

"You fellas lost?" A big red haired man asked.

"Yea, we are, as a matter of fact," I answered.

"Well, climb out and have some grub with us," he added.

After we ate, I had a question. "Where are your Immortals?"

They all looked at each other and smiled.

"We don't have any here," a small black haired guy answered.

I was somewhat shocked but in a way I liked that. No Immortals here. Could this place be hidden even from them?

[N.D.] The next day we were invited to take part in the "games."

We discovered that the men here regularly divided into groups. These groups would spread into the surrounding mountains and seek to defeat each other in physical competition. Cliff and I joined the team of the large red haired man who first greeted us. There seemed to be few rules except that the camp at the base of the valley floor was neutral territory.

We had been out for four nights when we first engaged another team. I was given a heavy stick which was weighted on one end. Some of my other team members had knives and even a few old pre-reign exploding weapons. I began to wonder how serious these games were. We found our opposing team just before sunrise. The battle was furious. Many were seriously wounded and some were killed outright. However, our team had won. I was in a state of shock. I confronted our leader, himself seriously wounded and bleeding from the head and from one side.

"This is wrong," I said. "What is the point of it?"

"The point, Mark, is to win. We are warriors You don't like it?"

"Like it. It's barbaric. If the Immortals find out, you will all be executed."

"Yes, maybe. We are hard to find."

"Cliff and I are leaving."

"No, you're not. No one leaves. You are in for life here, man."

I reported this conversation to Cliff and we decided to go along with it until we could escape. I started taking long walks in the wilderness by myself when I could and called out for Lucius. He did not appear.

The next battle nine days later did not go as well for us. We were outnumbered and soon realized that we could not win. Many on my team attempted to surrender but were killed. Cliff and I were hiding under a ledge and believed that we had escaped detection. We moved out from our cover seeking a better place to hide and were jumped by over a dozen of the enemy team. I was flat on my back with a huge man sitting on me. He had a long knife poised over my chest. He raised it to strike and I closed my eyes. Surely this was the end of my mortal life. The next second my attacker was gone and I was still alive. I opened my eyes to see Lucius hovering over me.

"Where have you been?" I shouted.

Lucius smiled gently. Good old Lucius.

Cliff and I helped each other up. A very large contingent of angels had arrived. I was so grateful. Suddenly, Elaine appeared in front of me. I was never so glad to see someone in my life. I actually knelt before her.

"Is this the kind of life you want?" she asked calmly.

"No, Ma'am. Man without the government of the Reign is too destructive."

"Good boy." She clasped me on the shoulder.

"You knew about this all along."

"The Over-Lord here allowed it to operate. When you started in this direction, we decided to use it."

"I renew my loyalty to you and the Metropolitan and the Emperor, Elaine," I said. "I will be faithful." Elaine hugged me long and hard. This was indeed a first for me. She is an attractive woman somewhat smaller than I am. I was so glad to see her. I am well aware that a mortal male can not have a personal relationship with an Immoral female. I introduced my new friend, Cliff, to her.

"Cliff, this is my governor, the Immortal Elaine." She smiled and nodded.

"It is an honor, Excellency," Cliff answered.

"I want to go home, Elaine, I have work to do," I said.

"Cliff, do you want to come with me?"

"I believe I will go home too, Mark, thanks."

Cliff started for home in the old vehicle. I went back with Lucius and Elaine.

05.17.160 C.R. After I had rested from my ordeal, I went to pay my respects to the Metropolitan. He was glad to see me. He said that I have changed. Then I divided mother's writings into groups and started to read them all again. About two months into this task Elaine surprised me with a visit. I had not worried about not seeing her since I returned.

"Elaine, dear mistress," I almost dashed into her arms.

"You are looking fine, Mark."

"Take refreshments with me?" I asked.

I brought out some fruit and cheese. Elaine always seemed to enjoy her food. I am not sure myself if they actually need to eat, but they seem to enjoy it.

She seemed to have a secret. After we ate and visited, she smiled.

"I have someone else to see you," she said. She stepped into a portal for a few seconds and returned with Martha. She was a wonderful sight for my eyes.

"We had to ask Martha to step aside for a while during your travels, Mark. But she has now told us that she would like to see you again."

I hugged Martha for a long time. She felt so good to me. Elaine had slipped away. I took Martha to my cousins nearby to stay and we have been seeing each other regularly.

09.11.160 C.R.   I remember the accounts of my parent's wedding in mother's journal. I wondered what ours would be like. I asked Elaine for permission which she promptly gave and we set a date for three months later. Martha's father is dead but her mother is very supportive. We planned to have the ceremony at my house and sent out the invitations. About two months before the wedding Elaine appeared at my house.

"It is good to see you, Excellency," I said.

"Excellency? You are formal today, Mark."

"Sorry, Elaine. It is good to see you. I have missed you."

"And I have missed you, my young friend." She took my hand.

Elaine continued, "The Metropolitan wants to do the ceremony."

"That's great, at the Dais?"

"No, actually. Here at your residence."

"Residence?"

"Yes, here at your house, your residence."

Residence sounded rather official. But I was very happy. As far as I know, the Metropolitan had never performed a marriage in the home of a mortal. I am not even sure that he has even visited the home of a mortal. My exclusion must be over.

When the day actually came, I had forgotten that the Metropolitan did not travel anywhere without his angelic escort, even the short distance from the Dais to my house.

This really highlighted our wedding in a way that I had not foreseen. Just as my mother had said, the Immortals truly love weddings.

The ceremony was to begin at ten in the morning. Martha, with her mother's help, had made a beautiful dress. It was in the traditional white but ingeniously designed with an abundance of pre-Reign lace that had been in her family forever. I was just preparing to put on my best clothing when Elaine arrived with a robe such as I have never had before. It was designed similar to the robe of a civil magistrate like my grandfather would have worn on official occasions. However, it was not black but a brilliant shade of blue with white borders. If that was what Elaine wanted me to wear, then I would wear it. The arrival of the Metropolitan's escort captured the attention of our guests. My house and gardens were packed with people. The Metropolitan arrived and took his position at the front of my large room where the ceremony was to take place. I stood beside him and we watched Martha enter. She threw me a quick look of surprise and approval when she saw my new robe. I felt very honored by the entire involvement of the Immortals. I knew that I was now fully accepted as mother's successor which made me both excited and frightened. We took our wedding trip to the tropical islands courtesy of Lucius; another action which caused no little notice from my mortal contemporaries.

[N.D.] A couple of weeks after we returned from our trip, I was deep in my work in my study when Elaine arrived in the study itself. I stood and rushed to her.

"You had a nice trip?"

It was poised as a question, but it may have been a statement. I still do not understand exactly what they know. Elaine, dear Elaine.

"Yes, Ma'am. Wonderful. The islands are beautiful, and my Martha is beautiful and tender."

"Yes, well, I died a virgin. So some things, my dear Mark, that you understand are beyond my experience."

All I could do was smile.

"Now to my intentions. Mark, I want to take you and Martha on a tour of some of the primary Dais' of the world."

I was surprised and pleased.

She continued, "You are a natural at your research like you mother was. We have no doubt that you will write it well and that your people will appreciate your work. All that lacks is that you become more familiar with the world. From then on Lucius will be permitted to take you to various areas to speak on your research."

I nodded obediently.

"Good, please prepare to depart in three days. It will take several weeks. Now, if I may visit Martha?" She departed my study. Had she implied that my permission was a factor? I would have to think about this. It also seems that Martha is in considerable favor. This is a new era for my family.

The tour was fabulous and there is certainly more to our beloved Elaine than being Governor of Buckhead in the court of Henry Sawyer, Metropolitan of Atlanta. We went everywhere with an escort of nearly half a legion. I am certainly fortunate to have Lucius alone to precede me, but as under governor, Elaine does not rate a half Legion. Perhaps they are representatives of the Metropolitan, but the more we travel the more I doubt that. Of the many Metropolitans, Governors and Over-Lords that we are meeting, this size of this escort is still extraordinary.

We went from Atlanta to Rio. From there we went to Brasilia, then Bogotá, then Mexico City, then Conception. From there we went West to Tokyo, Bangkok and Seoul, then to Peking and Moscow. By then we were going East and I had hopes for Jerusalem but that was not to happen. I actually let Elaine know that I was disappointed but there was no response. Perhaps not even she can go to the Imperial capitol without being bidden but I doubt that. Martha is loving it and has a very refined presence. She is certainly the right wife for me. From Moscow we visited the Dais' in Berlin, Paris, Brussels, Madrid, Vienna, Budapest, Athens and Rome. I was surprised, due to my familiarity with pre-Reign history, that Rome did not seem to have any special significance during the Reign. Jerusalem is everything pertaining to the Emperor. Then down to New Delhi and Nairobi and Johannesburg but we did not stop at Jerusalem. Then we went West again to Boston, Toronto, New York (this time in my official status) where I greeted the Over-Lord Janice with a special enthusiasm, then on to Philadelphia, Washington then West to Denver, Houston, and Los Angeles. What a spectacular trip. At each Dais Elaine would sit next to the ruler and I would sit on the grass beside her with Lucius behind me. Mostly I would listen to the affairs of that court but sometimes I would be asked about my work. Soon I began to give the same answers at each place.

"Yes, my Lord, the work is going well. . . . Yes, my people in their generations need to know the ancient books and the history of your generations. . . . Yes, sir, there is good response most everywhere. . . . Yes, Ma'am, I am proud to be involved. . . . Yes, Elaine is a wonderful inspiration to me and to my wife." On and on it went.

As I have mentioned, I was particularly struck with Rome. The Metropolitan there is one Luigi Patroni. He is a stout man with dark black curls, most typical of the people there. His court is no different than most that I visited, no grander or larger. I did discover in my research there that most of the Metropolitans have considerable libraries of pre-Reign books that were salvaged and a few from the Reign itself. I do plan to visit many of them with Lucius' help and Elaine says that I will be welcomed. I also discovered that the Metropolitan of Rome had actually been a Pope near the end of mortal times and he had stood as a witness for the Emperor and that he had been executed in a terrible manner by the evil authorities. As an ancient martyr for the Emperor he was, therefore, qualified to be Metropolitan, but not because of his status at the time.

02.22.165 C.R.   The Over-Lord of Eastern Europe, Perpetua, was martyred at a very young age just after the Emperor had come as a man and accomplished his Glorious work and returned to His Father. After she was captured, she was tortured but was soon seen comforting and praying for the other prisoners. They then hung her upside down from a pole and loosed some lions on her but the lions would not approach as they feared her angels which the Lions could see but the mortals could not see. Finally, they sewed her into a bag and threw her under a stampeding herd of cattle and she died. She was about 13 years of age when she died but now she is said to rule with wisdom. This trip has allowed me to observe Immortals worldwide and I have formed many new certainties about them.

Now all of the Immortals appear to be about the same age. Their bodies show no sign of age no matter what age they were when they died. They all appear to be in their early thirties, the age of the Emperor when He died. Their faces also look about the same age. However, if you look closely, there is sometimes a clue as to the age that they died in their faces. Those who died younger have a certain youthful look in their faces and those who died in old age have a certain appearance of maturity in their faces. They recognize each other by facial features as we do. On this trip I believe that I observed Immortals meeting who have not met as Immortals before. Their present faces bear enough similarity with their mortal faces that they can recognize each other at the first encounter after the change if they were acquainted as mortals. But there are no signs of injury or the effects of disease on their person in any way. If they lost limbs or were disfigured as mortals, they are always restored. For the most part we do not understand the difference between their bodies and ours. We grow old and die; they do not. We can bleed; they do not. We can be injured; they can not. We can become ill; they can not. When we do become ill, they usually heal us so there is no need for physicians although some mortals still study the mortal body. Their flesh is warm as is ours. They have bones within as we do. They never appear to be overweight as some mortals are. They show no interest in sexual matters and they do not reproduce. As far as we know, they do not sleep, or at least no mortal has ever seen them sleep. We do not know what they do when they are "away." Their greatest joy seems in being "away" with the Emperor. All these things are true for the princes as well as the other Immortals. Those who do not rule seem to spend more time off the earth. We are not sure that their internal parts function as ours do. Their physical being is said to be the same as that of the Emperor except that He has chosen to retain the wounds that He suffered. Also, the Emperor, I am told, always has a subtle divine aura around Him which consists of both a bright but gentle light and various sweet smells.

04.21.166 C.R. Each Dais that I visited on the trip was slightly different but equally beautiful. Always, the site was one of importance in mortal times and often the scene of some persecution of the Immortals who were both servants and siblings of the Emperor. They seemed to rejoice in celebrating their mortal persecutions for the Emperor. In every case the Dais had been naturalized, whatever structure or symbol had existed there was removed or leveled and a grassy Dais was created with the usual white chairs arranged in a semicircle. During the day the sun always shines if the ruler is on the Dais. That too seems to be under Imperial control.

In Rio the Dais is under the enormous pre-Reign statue of the Emperor. They glory in that. In Moscow it is in the midst of the Kremlin. In London it is in front of Westminster Abbey and in Paris it is in front of Notre Dame. Only in Rome does the Metropolitan seem to have been a person who was well known during his time. But by then he was the head of a persecuted minority. In every other place the ruler was a "nobody" in mortal life. The Emperor sees importance different than we do. The Over-Lord of Western Europe was an unknown, Stefan Heicht, and he reigns from the Dais in Brussels. The Over-Lord in Peking, Li Chen, was a slave as a mortal. He was mistreated by a series of masters for his faith in the Emperor and was killed by being tied hand and foot and thrown to a pack of mad dogs. Now he is a very happy little man who laughs almost constantly. Each court, each Dais, each ruler is unique and equally beautiful. This trip has changed my perspective forever. I have much to consider and to study and to write.

06.22.166 C.R.   Upon our return from this world tour Elaine took us directly to the Dais of our Metropolitan, Henry. He asked me about the trip and seemed satisfied with my answers. Even though I traveled with Elaine and Lucius which is immediate and easy, both Martha and I were still tired from the trip. Another thing the Immortals do not experience. The Metropolitan obviously recognized my fatigue and kindly dismissed us early to go to our house, pardon, our residence and rest. It was good to be alone with Martha without so much fear of interruption. Although the trip had been a great learning experience for both of us, it had not done a lot for our relationship.

[N.D.]   I had not been to the Dais as often as I should have. I determined to attend more often. Usually I just observed, but I always thought that attendance was expected since Mother attended and watched often.

"It is good to see you at the Dais more often," Elaine said.

"It is good to be here. I have been too often absent."

"Why the change?"

"It,   it   is   expected.   Isn't   it?"

"Perhaps expected but not required."

"Mother came so often. I practically grew up here."

"Your Mother came because she loved to be here."

I looked around. "I grew up with it. But, I will be here more often."

She took my hand and led me to the Metropolitan.

"Henry, look who's here," she said.

"Mark, welcome. We see too little of you," the Metropolitan said.

"You   shall   see   more   of   me,   Excellency,"   I responded.

07.01.166 C.R.   I began to become interested with the judgments that were passed by the Metropolitan and the others. When the Metropolitan was away, Elaine would usually fill in at the daily court. Sometimes one of the other rulers under Henry Sawyer would have the daily docket. All sorts of cases came before them from high treason against the Emperor to domestic disputes and once in a while even an animal cruelty charge. All of life was under the purview of the Immortal princes.

08.09.166 C.R.   On one particularly slow afternoon when Elaine was in charge a certain husband was brought before the Dais. The two angels who brought him were ordinary angels like Lucius.

"This man has been abusing his wife," they reported.

"What are the particulars?" Elaine asked.

"They have been married for almost two years. He never attends her. He is usually somewhere becoming intoxicated with his male companions. He is 20 years of age and she is 18 years of age. Her mother is their only living parent; she abides with them. This man often comes home and beats his wife."

"Where is the wife?" Elaine asked.

"Do you require her, Excellency?" one of the angels asked.

"Yes, bring her." That angel departed.

The accused stood there with a surly look. Occasionally he would glance at Elaine herself in a leering disrespectful manner. She would return his gaze firmly. Still he did not stop.

"Your name," Elaine demanded.

"Sam," he shot back.

The angel arrived with the wife. She was an attractive girl. Her clothes were tattered but clean. And older woman, I presumed to be her mother, was with her. She was with child. She was obviously frightened.

"Sit down, child," Elaine said softly. A female mortal court attendant brought a chair and help her to sit. Another chair was brought for her mother.

"What is your name, child," Elaine asked.

"Mary," she answered.

"Oh, such a special name! Does this man abuse you?" Elaine asked.

She looked at him. He leered back a warning. She did not speak.

"Listen to me, girl," Elaine said, still softly. "You may fear him, but I promise he will hurt you no more. However, it is required that you answer me."

"Ya, ah er, yes, Excellency. He, . . . beats me." She did not look back at her husband. Elaine came forward to examine her bruises. Her left eye was swollen shut and badly blackened. There was an older greener bruise on her right cheek. Her arms had several bruises. When Elaine touched her back lightly, she winced.

"Are you bruised here too?" Elaine asked.

The woman shook her head. Elaine pulled up her blouse a little and looked at her back.

"Oh, darling, that is terrible. Where else do you have bruises?"

The woman pointed to most of her body.

"Why did you marry him?" Elaine asked.

"I was told to do so, Excellency." She glanced toward her mother.

"Why?" Elaine looked directly at the mother.

"We had nothing, Excellency," the mother answered. "His father gave me some gold. It seemed the best thing to do at the time."

"Now he is dead?"

"Yes, he drank himself to death."

"And this man does not provide?"

"No, no, he does not," the mother answered looking defiantly at the man.

"Why?" Elaine stepped forward a few paces and looked the man in the eyes.

"Well, she, . . she is no good, mistress," he said.

"No good? How?"

"She just complains and she doesn't meet my needs since, since she got that way."

"And just who got her that way?"

He shrugged. "Me, I guess."

"You know it was you, you slacker," the mother interjected. "She would never go with anyone else." Then the mother looked nervously at Elaine for fear that she had spoken out of turn.

"The child is yours and she has many healed fractures of her bones. Come here," Elaine said to the man.

With this knowledge revealed he shuffled forward. He looked Elaine up and down. I shivered.

"This is your wife," Elaine continued. "It is your duty to care for her even if you are not capable of loving her. She is carrying your child. Is there no work in your area?"

"Nothing I like to do," he blurted back.

"And just what would be to your liking?" Elaine asked. "Do not bother to answer. You are a foul man."

He jerked towards Elaine.

An angel appeared between them faster than I could see him move. I knew that he could not actually harm Elaine, but such actions are not allowed.

Elaine walked over to the girl. They spoke in hushed tones for a short time. The girl would glance in her husband's direction from time to time. The mother strained to hear what was being said. Elaine took the girl's hands in hers and looked into her eyes. Then she stood.

"I find you inexcusable," she said to Sam. "I judge your character to be hopelessly twisted."

"I have resources for you, Mary," Elaine said. "Near my residence. You will stay there until your child is born and then I will see that you are better established."

The mother moved towards Elaine, but Elaine put her hand out for her to stop.

"As for you," Elaine addressed the mother, "you are not much of a mother. There are always abundant facilities for the needy. This is the Imperial Reign. You should not have sold your child to this wretched man."

"Hey," the man objected.

Elaine picked up her scepter from the table next to her seat. The man recognized this and got quiet.

"You may accompany your daughter, woman. But I will have you watched. Strive to improve." Elaine commanded. The woman bowed her head.

"Now as for you," Elaine addressed the man. "I only need one more reason to remove you altogether."

"Do you think I am afraid of you?" the man challenged.

"You should have been," Elaine said softly as she raised her scepter. She spun the pointed end towards him. He looked as if he was getting ready to spit on her. But then he grasped his throat and fell to the ground.

"He is dead," Elaine said. The mother fell to her knees and the girl gasped.

Elaine looked at the girl. She showed no sorrow at the death of her husband.

"I rather think you will do better as a widow," Elaine said. "There are many good men in this world. But this was not one of them," she said looking down at the body as if it were some sort of waste. She pointed the scepter again and the body was gone. The girl and her mother were shown away by a mortal aide.

Elaine replaced her scepter on the little table and sat down and everyone was very quiet for a few minutes, mortal and Immortal alike. Elaine crossed her legs and looked out onto the great expanse of park lands that stretched in front of the Dais. Carol, the Prince of Decatur, another under governor, leaned towards Elaine and touched her hand.

"It was the best thing to do," Carol said.

"I know. And I can remember the time when I could not have done it," Elaine responded.

"Me too," Carol said. They grasped each others hands for a moment.

Even at the Dais the taking of a life is no light thing. I believed that this man could have lived if he had been more respectful, but maybe it was not in him. At any rate, gross disrespect for an Immortal Prince is a dangerous activity. This is when it first came home to me that the Immortals grew in their abilities too. Ruling and judging seemed to come so easily to the Metropolitan. Today I saw my mistress grow in strength and integrity.

"Mark," Elaine said.

"Yes," I responded.

She motioned me near so I approached and hunkered down beside her.

She asked me to consider a program where Martha and I would meet with couples, especially the younger ones, and talk of marital duties and the like. I told her we would start planning it immediately. She seemed some happier. After the Metropolitan returned, he affirmed Elaine in her decision and made it clear that such ill treatment would not be allowed in his realm or in any of the realms of the Emperor.

02.19.167 C.R.   Martha and I have been speaking all over the world on the joys of married life. It is not difficult to do because she is such a dear wife and I love her very much. I told the men that it was their duty and privilege to honor and protect their wives. I reminded them that many couples fall in love after they marry. Even though Martha and I were in love before our marriage was arranged, my mother Anna fell in love with my father after they were married. I assured them, that in any event, the abuse of a wife would not be permitted under the Reign and I told them the story of poor Mary's husband. I encouraged parents not to force their daughters into marriage but to consult an Immortal instead. It was then that a thought hit me. Could we ask the Emperor for permission to designate certain Immortals who did not have ruling duties to counsel the mortals? I put it at the head of my list to talk to Elaine about at our next regular conference. Martha would tell the women to honor their husbands and that just as a husband should cover and protect his wife, the wife should cover and protect him against temptation and other women by being supportive and willingly participating in their intimate relationships. We have given many examples about putting your spouse's interests above your own from our own marriage and have asked others to share.

05.12.167 C.R.   My request for personal and marriage counselors has been sent to the Emperor. Elaine says that it will be discussed in their private fellowships.

03.23.168 C.R.   Something that I noticed on this recent tour is that some Metropolitan's have a Deputy Metropolitan. I have noticed this in the past but I did not deem it important enough to put in my journal. I have decided to include it here. This title may be a little misleading because the Deputy Metropolitan does not rule for the Metropolitan in his absence. Other under governors or Princes like Elaine and Carol do this for every Metropolitan. The Deputy handles many cases in symphony with the Metropolitan himself. There is usually a Deputy in areas where long term hate feuds have existed among the mortals for centuries. Since our mortals are still susceptible to such things, they have to be dealt with in a special way. I noticed several Deputy situations on this tour. The Deputy is highly respected and is almost as an equal to the Metropolitan.

08.11.168 C.R.   The Metropolitan of Oklahoma City is Billy Three Feathers. His Deputy is Bill Carson. Their Dais is on top of a mountain where the Sun shines very brightly and almost continuously. They have ordered a small bright cloud to always stay between the Dais and the sun for the benefit of mortals at or around the Dais. The sunlight seems to have no ill effect on the Immortals even those with a fair skin color. They are always happy to tell their story so I record it here. It seems that Bill Carson was an officer in the famous death march called the "trail of tears" where most of Billy Three Feathers' tribe, men, women and children, were death marched from far in the east by the national army of that day. Three Feathers was not quite a man then, only a boy of 12. Carson required Three Feathers to carry his personal baggage and spoke very roughly to the boy. The boy was a believer in the Emperor as most of his tribe had been for some time.

After several weeks Carson thought that he had worn the boy out so he ordered another young man to carry the heavy baggage. Three Feathers would not have it. He said that he was strong enough and that he would carry it all the way if necessary. This was in obedience to the then invisible Emperor's command. Three Feathers was so helpful and cheerful that he actually won Carson over to being a believer in the Emperor. Three Feathers was a constant witness to the Emperor all of his life for which he suffered considerable persecution. Later Carson went to another tribe not too far away as a missionary to tell them about the Emperor. After only three months he was captured and burned to death by this tribe, but he would not deny the Emperor. At the Return of the Emperor Three Feathers was made Metropolitan and Carson was made his deputy. They both rule in all things and put another Prince in charge when they leave to travel or to be with the Emperor. The Metropolitan and the Deputy are always together. So they are both ruling and judging in any case where their two individual mortal peoples are in conflict, which is quite often. This way this old hate feud is disarmed and the mortals know that they must appear before both of them. Surely the Emperor's wisdom is beyond compare. They even joke around the Dais about "Big Bill" and "Little Billy." "Little Billy" is the Metropolitan. "Big Bill" is his Deputy and they love each other dearly.

Mark

The Metropolitan of Johannesburg in South Africa is Joseph Kuboto, his Deputy is Helmut de Klerk. Their mortal peoples are ancient enemies and still tend to be that way even under the Reign. Kuboto and de Klerk are famous in the Empire for their wisdom in healing the divisions. They have declared their peoples all to be brothers and any harm inflicted by either side is atoned for with individual service to the other side. They have even had people tied together with an angelic rope until they learned to help each other. This rope is usually invisible and can not be loosed except by a command of the Metropolitan and his Deputy or the Emperor Himself.

Even though the Emperor has his earthly palace and temple in Jerusalem that city also has a Metropolitan of its own, and a Deputy. The Metropolitan of Jerusalem is Ehud Stein, the Deputy is Abdul Al Ibrahim. They did not live at the same time so they did not know each other then. They both converted to faith in the Emperor and were killed for their faith. They lovingly but firmly require their separate mortal peoples to work in unity and good faith with each other. Mercy is administered by both to mortals on both sides and judgment, sometimes harsh judgment, is dispensed by both the Metropolitan and the Deputy to mortals of both sides equally. There are other Metropolitan and Deputy Metropolitan teams in the world. I am interested in getting all of their stories. There are an unusual number of Deputy Metropolitans along the river Bosrus from Istanbul on the Mediterranean Sea all the way North as there are many ancient feuds along this famous East-West border. Our own Metropolitan of Atlanta does not have a deputy, but Henry Sawyer himself is from the prominent "minority" there.

[N.D.] It has been a long time since my requests for counselors went to the Emperor and Elaine now tells me that there have been many volunteers among the Immortals who do not have ruling responsibilities to do this. Several will be assigned to every Dais in the world. They will be there always and clearly identified as Family Counselors with a silver medallion with two interlocking rings engraved on it on a blue ribbon around their necks. If they are all busy and more are needed, more will be sent for right away. I am very happy about this. I wonder why this has not been thought of before by an Immortal or the Emperor. Martha says it is because it was my place to do so. I feel humbled with the responsibilities of my office.

01.11.169 C.R. When we awoke the day after we returned from our recent trip, I got some food from the kitchen and went directly to my study. Where to start? I reviewed many of the old manuscripts and started to put them in stacks in order of priority. Martha interrupted.

"Look, Mark, who's here!"

I turned to see the smiling face of our old friend Cliff.

"Cliff, what a treat. Welcome. Welcome."

We shared a manly embrace.

"Doesn't he look wonderful, Mark?"

"Yes, indeed, he does."

"Say, I am really sorry that I missed your wedding. I hear that it was quite something. I just could not get away. My Mom was not doing well at all, and . . . she died last month."

We both assured him of our sympathies. Death is still always alien to us and we do not know what lies on the other side as the Immortals did. We just concentrate on trusting the Emperor's judgment in the matter.

"So I thought I would travel some and visit you. You are the only important person that I know, Mark."

I did not say that I am not important but I brushed it aside by moving on.

"Wonderful, stay as long as you will. We will have a good time together."

Later I learned that Cliff also had another motive for visiting us.

About that time Cliff saw Lucius standing nearby. He nodded nervously to Lucius. "Ah, you have to go somewhere?" Cliff asked.

"No, not as far as I know." I looked at Lucius. He indicated nothing. "Don't mind him," I said. "He will express himself when he wants to and he would never hurt you."

Cliff nodded.

01.13.169 C.R. A few days later Cliff and I were sitting in my garden drinking some juice. I could tell that he had something that he wanted to talk about.

"Say, Mark, old man."

"Yes."

"I very nearly got into trouble in the months after I left you."

"How   so?"

"Well, I had intended to go home, but I started traveling instead. I traveled alone."

"I'm listening."

"I fell in with a group in Canada that don't really recognize the authority of the Emperor. They don't actually do anything illegal. But they meet and talk about human rights and are planning to petition the Emperor for more judicial authority at the mortal level. A lot of them have studied some pre-Reign law. At first I thought their arguments were sound. But they started to sound angry and very vocal, so I left."

"So far nothing too serious," I said.

"Really?"

"Really, the Emperor is always open to seeing how well we can govern ourselves. That is so long as our self government is still submissive to His appointed Governors."

"After the way the Immortals and their angels put down that group that we fell in with, I thought that these lawyers might be in real trouble."

"Not necessarily. Do you think you could find them again?"

"I don't think they would have moved. If they haven't already been disciplined, or something."

I looked at Lucius. He nodded.

"Lucius will take us to them," I said.

"Uh, do we need Elaine?"

Not a bad idea I thought.

"Lucius I need to see Elaine," I said.

Lucius disappeared and we waited for about 5 minutes when he returned with Elaine. I stood and Cliff bowed deeply. I gestured toward a chair for Elaine. I offered her a drink and she accepted. We repeated Cliff's report to her. I started and asked Cliff to join in. She listened and then told me to investigate in my official role which would merely indicate my interest in what they were doing. She did not comment if they were already under scrutiny for anything else. Elaine and I hugged. Cliff bowed and she departed. I was glad that Elaine does not normally bring her angelic retinue with her to my house as she did to my wedding; Cliff might have gone into shock.

Martha said that she would like to remain at home. She has had an upset stomach especially in the mornings. Cliff and I talked for quite a while and departed the next morning.

01.15.169 C.R. The meeting was interrupted by our appearance. Lucius did not change his form, but the appearance of an angel and of us coming through a portal

71

had a definite effect. Many of the group looked rather sheepish. The one who was speaking and the chairman looked confident. I introduced myself.

"We know who you are," the chairman said.

"We have come only to listen. I am a mortal just as you are."

"A mortal perhaps, but not as we are." The speaker said.

"I am as you are. Prick me, do I not bleed?"

I thought for a moment that they were going to take me literally but they did not.

"Cliff has brought him to us," one young woman added.

"I bring you no trouble," Cliff answered.

"And him?" the chairman asked looking at Lucius.

"He does my bidding," I said boldly but I could not resist glancing toward Lucius after I said it. He showed no change in demeanor so I had gotten away with it.

After several more exchanges we persuaded them to continue their discussion. They even offered us seats. What they now wanted to do was to petition the Emperor to establish a mortal magistrate to judge the more minor civil matters, cases involving non-violent conflict between mortals. To date all judgments are handed down by Immortals. Cliff whispered to me that their discussions had progressed considerably since he had been with them and that some of the angrier ones were no longer there. I replied that they were better off with these absences and that those angry ones would no doubt be dealt with eventually by the Immortal courts. Later I went aside to speak to Lucius then I dispatched him on an errand. I was content that I was safe with these people. They seemed sincere and rational. Cliff began to enter into the discussion and he showed considerable insight and wisdom. When Lucius returned and reported to me, I asked for a chance to be heard. The chair agreed.

"My Governor, Elaine, assures me that when your case is complete, she will take it to the Emperor."

They were all surprised and very happy. I left Cliff there at his request and returned home. I was concerned about my wife. As it turned out, there was no need for concern. We are to have a child. Martha wanted to know if it was a boy or a girl. She asked Elaine and she said that it was a boy. We plan to name him Carl.

[N.D.]   Three months after I met with the lawyers, Cliff contacted me that they were ready. I informed Elaine. Elaine contacted the Metropolitan of Boston and received his blessing to visit the group. She took me and Lucius and her angelic escort. She was welcomed in the most tasteful of fashions. The advocates, Cliff told me that they wanted to be known as advocates, had foreseen Elaine's escort so they set up a large garden for the reception with that in mind. Everyone from several principalities that was interested in this new mortal court was present; several thousand, I estimated. Seats had been set up facing the platform. I arrived with Elaine and Lucius on the platform just behind Elaine's escort. Everyone stood when the portal appeared. The escort passed in front of us and spread themselves out over the platform and the garden in the usual fashion. Elaine followed her escort. Lucius preceded me as I stepped through from my study. I did not see Elaine leave the Metropolitan's Dais. I just waited for Lucius to open my portal as he did not need one and it was all angelically coordinated in perfect timing.

We were welcomed by their chairman and a few others including Cliff. It seemed like Cliff had become quite involved. He had told me that he was studying legal procedure. They explained to Elaine the entire structure that they were petitioning from the Emperor. She assured them that one of her angels had recorded every word and instructed them to meet her at this same platform in two weeks. In two weeks we returned and the crowd in attendance had more than doubled. It seemed to me that the Metropolitan had added to Elaine's escort with some from his own. It struck me that Elaine does considerably more with mortals than any other governor that I had met.

Elaine proclaimed, "The mortal civil Magistrate is established. You will need to elect your own officers to serve until a larger part of the population is involved. The Imperial publishers have been instructed to give you all necessary aid. As you develop your system and procedures, you will designate a group of three to report and coordinate with me. You will contact me at the Dais of the Metropolitan of Atlanta by letter. All the Immortals will recognize this mortal court as having appropriate jurisdiction over mortal matters. All decisions are subject to review by the Princes of the earth. Capital matters will remain under the authority of the Princes alone."

Everyone stood and applauded and cheered for a very long time. I wondered if they knew what they were getting into. It seemed to me that the Imperial Reign with all the Immortal ruler judges was working just fine. Evidently the Emperor was content to allow these advocates to create and maintain this subordinate system. The entire system took about a decade to spread throughout the earth. By that time Cliff was the Chief Magistrate of the mortal court. The official language of the court was old American, chosen in order to reduce the need for translators. The Immortals spoke all earthly languages innately and Elaine told me that the Emperor's own language in its ancient form is the only one spoken at court.

[N.D.] Cliff married another advocate, Mary, and they visit us often at the residence. There is no conflict between Cliff's office and mine. My work is directly under Imperial control and I confer exclusively with Elaine. My work is to study and inspire and lead, not to settle petty conflicts. However, I indicated to Cliff that I respect his work which is all consuming to him. A quiet afternoon with Elaine is more to my liking and now Martha is usually with us unless I have some important issues pertaining to my work to discuss. Sometimes the three of us just sit in silence and enjoy the garden with its many flowers and birds. Our gardener is excellent at his work. I once asked Elaine during one of these afternoons if she wouldn't rather be "off world" with the Immortals.

She responded, "Our fellowship is wonderful and the closer a person gets to the Emperor the better it becomes. But there are many of us, more than you mortals. We have many generations revived among us. I love you two and little Carl very much." That was enough for us. We were always honored to be with her and she had such a sweet personality that it was refreshing to be near her.

I asked her, "Elaine, what do you mean when you say that the fellowship gets better the closer one gets to the Emperor. I have never seen the Emperor, but I hear that his presence is often overwhelming."

"It may be difficult to communicate," Elaine answered. "We communicate, fellowship, at a different level. Most of the time we do not have to talk. We either know what each other is thinking or we speak mind to mind, actually more heart to heart. Mostly we enjoy each other much like we three enjoy each other here in the garden. Our hearts meet each other and share the joy of life."

"But your life is different from ours," I interrupted.

"Yes, some different, but all life is given by the Emperor and His Father, and His Presence."

"You have His Presence within you; but we do not."

"We have His Presence internally. We had Him that way as mortals. But He is still among you. He is the essence of love."

"Let me try to understand this," I continued. "Then you, Immortals . . . commune, is that a good word?" She nodded. I went on, "you commune with each other as living beings, and all life comes from the Emperor and the Father, and His Presence, uh, enhances this communing?"

"Exactly."

"Then how does being close to the Emperor further enhance your communing?"

"A very perceptive question, Mark. I am so proud of you."

I suppose if I live to be ninety years old, an expression of pride from this "33 year old" Immortal will always thrill my heart. I know that I was smiling from ear to ear. "Well, how? Dear Elaine?"

"The Emperor has a unique relationship with His Father. Even we can not actually see the Father. I will not expand on that. When we are near the Emperor, this relationship that They have mixes with and overwhelms our relationships, even that which we have in His Presence away from His body, and carries us to an entirely new level. It is ecstasy; it is pure joy; it is indescribable. "

" Is what we share here even the tiniest part of that?" I asked.

"Yes, Mark, yes, it is."

We did not speak for a long time. The garden seemed even more beautiful.

10.16.204 C.R. Carl was ten years old today. Elaine came to his party as did Cliff and all of our local friends and many from other areas of Janice's realm and even a few from other places in the world. Carl is a fine boy. He is big and strong for his age and has beautiful thick blond hair. Sometimes he can be willful, but he is usually obedient. Martha has trained him well and I often wish that I could spend more time with him. I have resolved to do so from now through his teen years. I asked Elaine if she thought my work would suffer too much for it.

"Absolutely not, Mark," Elaine answered. "Your duties as a father come before your work."

"Before?"

"Yes, your work will take care of itself."

I am confirmed. I will spend a lot more time with Carl. We have not been blessed with other children as yet. Martha tends to worry about this, but I tell her to be at ease.

"Elaine, do you know if we will have any more children? Martha wants them so."

"Is she concerned?"

"Quite."

"Are you, how do you say, 'trying'?"

"Yes, I would say that we are."

Elaine motioned to Martha and she joined us.

"Do you want more children, dear?"

"Oh, yes, we do so much," Martha answered taking my hand in hers and looking at me lovingly.

"Then you shall," Elaine said and she touched Martha's stomach lightly and briefly.

"When will you two ever learn?" Elaine said. "You of all people. We can grant these things if you will only ask. Mark, as soon as you do your part she will conceive."

I have been doing my job for some years now and I am still amazed at what I learn. Why didn't we ask before?

[N.D.] Little Anna was born nine months and one week later. She is beautiful and Martha and I and Carl love her dearly. Carl is wonderful with her and very protective. Even Lucius seems happy when he is around her.

[N.D.] Today is Carl's wedding. He is 19 and little Anna is 12. She will be a bridesmaid. Carl's bride is named Toni and she is a beautiful girl, very petite with jet black hair and alabaster skin. She is very conscientious and helpful. Martha and I like her very much. Carl met her at his advanced school where he has studied human nature. We are quite a happy family and I am honored to serve as I do.

3 * May

338 - 358

01.10.338 C.R. My name is May. I am the fifth in succession in the Annatic line. I am 18 years old today. I was invested with my titles today.   I am the daughter of Alice, the fourth in succession. I am the Keeper of the Ancient Books, the Primary Interpreter of the books of Anna, and the Chronicler of Imperial truth. My parents are both dead. Father died when I was four years old and my mother, Alice, died when I was 12. Mother was 58 when she conceived me and 59 when I was born. She was enabled to do this by the miraculous intervention of our Governor, the Immortal Elaine. Elaine held my offices open for six years until I was considered old enough to take up the duties. This is unusual and had to be approved by the Emperor Himself who rules from Jerusalem. I love Him.

My babysitters have been the Immortal Elaine herself, ably assisted by my angel Lucius and my mother's faithful friend and secretary Margaret, "Maggie," Newhouse. Maggie was a widow of 2 years when my mother died. She was devoted to my mother and asked Elaine if she could continue to live at the Residence after my mother died to take care of me. They are my family, Maggie, Lucius, and Elaine; a mortal, an angel and an Immortal.

[N.D.] In my studies in preparing for my offices over the past six years I have learned a lot. Among the things that I have learned about are the ancient monastery rights of the followers of the then invisible Emperor during the Second Testament period between the first humble coming and the Glorious Return of His Imperial Majesty.

There were places for both men and women to live that existed primarily to enable the residents to become closer to the Emperor by what they called a life of "prayer and meditation." This "prayer" was the way that they communicated with the Emperor during his invisible time. Actually, the Emperor was "beyond the veil" with His Father and one called the Helper, a spiritual being and a part of God. The Helper would make communication with the Emperor possible through this "prayer and meditation." In praying they would talk to Him and in meditating they would listen for his voice. The men in these places, these monasteries, were called "monks" and the women, who had separate monasteries, were called "nuns." Our Over-Lord Janice was such a person when she was a mortal; she was a "nun." In addition to my studies in mother's magnificent library I interviewed Janice when I was 15 on this subject. I say that I "interviewed" her, but I do not think she felt that it was an interview. I asked Elaine if I could visit the Over-Lord's Dais and she gave me permission.

"Have you finished your studies for today, young lady?" Elaine asked.

"Yes, Ma'am. I have finished through next week as of today."

"I should have known. Go May, visit Janice. Give her my love."

I straightened by jumper and checked my hair and looked at Lucius. He opened a portal and we were gone. My visits to the Over-Lord's Dais were not unusual. So when we arrived, I just took a seat on the grass behind Janice. Janice likes me and it was never too long before she would turn and give me a big hug.

"May, darling. You are as sweet and pretty as ever," Janice said.

I blushed a little as usual and we shared a great big hug. She did not seem to be involved in anything at the time so I risked my first question.

"Janice!"

"Yes, May."

"I have been reading in the Second Testament, and I would like to ask you to help me clarify something," I said.

"Sure."

"What, . . . what exactly was it like to be a . . .nun?"

A few of the under governors looked around but Janice did not flinch.

"Well May, to be a nun meant that you lived a different life than most people. Your sisters in the monastery were your family. There was a Mother Superior. And we considered ourselves to be married to the Emperor. Only there was no physical relationship, only a spiritual one. Do you understand that? No sex."

"I understand; I am 15."

"Of course you are."

"Maggie told me everything when I was 13 and I have read some books that she recommended."

"Good, fine. Now, in the monastery we would cover all of our bodies and even our hair with what we called a . . ."

"Habit, it was a habit," I said. "Sorry, I interrupted."

"That's all right. Yes, it was a habit. Only our face and hands were uncovered. There was a starched type of frame around the face and a long flowing head covering. The dress went clear to the ground, the sleeves were long, extending down over our hands to our fingers. Our thumbs fit through a hole in the sleeve to hold the sleeve down. "

"How did you actually join this monastery?"

"We had a wedding. When we joined, we actually had a wedding ceremony to be married to the Emperor. As you know, He was invisible then."

I had been nodding my head so Janice continued.

"We brought Him our 'flame and our flower.' It was wonderful."

"Your flame and your flower?"

"Yes, child." Janice lowered her voice as if she was talking about something very sacred. "You see, in marrying the Emperor we were agreeing to hide our physical beauty and deny our physical passions for the rest of our lives. The flame was our passion and our flower was our beauty and our virginity. We carried one beautiful flower of our own choosing and a small white candle that was lit. We were dressed in a white wedding dress and we carried the flower and the candle to the altar, a holy table in the chapel, the church in our monastery. We placed the flower on the altar and blew out the candle and laid it next to it. Then we said our vows of love and faithfulness to the Emperor. After that we spent the night in prayer to Him and then the next morning we joined our sisters in our life of service and contemplation."

"Just what all did you do?"

"That depended on our 'order'. Some orders would teach children or run an orphanage. Some nursed the sick. Some were strictly contemplative. That means that all we did was pray to the Emperor and pray for people and sing in the choir. Sometimes the church, other believers, would pay for our needs and sometimes we would make something in the monastery that we could sell. Some even made wine to sell on the outside so that they could live the contemplative life."

I was still nodding.

"So," Janice said. "Do you understand?"

"Could I be the Keeper and also be a nun?"

"Well, . . . there are no nuns now dear. This is the Empire."

"I want to be married to the Emperor, spiritually, I mean. And, . . . be the keeper when I am old enough."

"We'll have to talk about this later, May."

"O.K."

Then Janice was needed for a judgment, so she turned around and I went over our talk in my mind. We did not talk about this again, but I did not forget a word. As I continued to study, in a year or so I verified from some writings everything that Janice had told me. It was not that I didn't believe her, I just wanted to read other accounts. I even found a copy of a wedding vow to the Emperor. I memorized it. I still intend to marry Him.

[N.D.] Now that I have been invested with my offices I intend to talk to Janice again. There has to be a way that this can be done. My life has no meaning unless I can wed the Emperor. I have devoted myself completely to Him and I will do my duties in my offices with my very best efforts for Him. I have chosen my particular flower. It is a white orchid with a very light blue border on the bloom and deep golden stamen. The candle, of course, will be white and the wick will be as long as possible to represent a large and hot flame. This I have and I will sacrifice it to Him along with all that I am or can be with His help. I have asked to see Janice tomorrow.

[N.D.] "May, little May," Janice greeted me.
"Janice, hello," I answered as we embraced. They, Janice and Elaine and even the Metropolitan Henry, have often called me 'little May' because I am barely five feet tall and I am slightly built. I have reddish hair which I wear back and they say that I am pretty. I wish that my hair was blond. I do not look 18, probably more like 14.
"You looked so mature at your investiture," Janice said. "I think that your Maggie altered Mark's robe wonderfully for you."
"She saved what she could not fold back," I said. "It will still be useful for others."
"Good, that's fine. This is your first visit to my Dais as Keeper. Welcome, Keeper May."
I bowed slightly. "Thank you, Over-Lord, I am honored to be here."

Janice smiled and just looked at me. We had taken care of the formalities. Everyone at the Dais was smiling. I sat with her most of the day waiting for my chance to talk privately and seriously. Finally, she rose and gestured for an under governor to preside. Eric moved from his place near the fringes and sat in her seat. Janice walked towards her residence at the Dais and I followed her. Once inside her private rooms she led me to her informal receiving room and had refreshments brought to us.

"You still like fresh lemonade?" Janice asked me.

"Yes, it is fine," I answered.

"You would prefer something else, Keeper?" she asked.

I understood that she was recognizing my passage to adulthood so I thought of something else to drink and the server went to get it all.

Janice knew what I was there to talk about. She had not forgotten. We talked for a long time. I went back three more times to talk about this. Finally, Janice said that the Emperor had agreed to a ceremony. I was surprised and deliriously happy.

The ceremony was to be this way. It would be held at the Dais of the Eastern Viceroy, John the Beloved at Patmos Island. I had chosen the place. I would have my white wedding dress and my flower and my flame. Afterwards I would wear a white habit covering everything but my face and my fingers that I designed after Janice's description of her habit when she was mortal and a picture I found in an old book. I would do all my duties as the Keeper as a wife of the Emperor. The Emperor was to send a very high angel to represent Him. This angel would wear a sunburst of gold, the Emperor's crest, and I would be given a ring for my wedding finger with an identical tiny sunburst and a gold chain for my neck with a slightly larger gold sunburst on it. I would use the vows that I had memorized when I was fifteen. These vows were known to

Elaine and Janice and had been communicated to the Emperor. The special angel would speak for Him. The date was set, six months from my investiture.

[N.D.] On the day I was at perfect peace. Two dozen of the orchids were floating in a basin in my room at Patmos. Several candles awaited and a large one was lit to provide the light for the one I was to carry. I took my choice of the orchids and the candles. It was a short walk to the Dais. At exactly Noon on Patmos I emerged from my room. I rushed to the table before the Viceroy where a magnificent angel awaited facing the Viceroy. I had to shield the candle with my other hand to protect the flame. The wick was long and the flame was high. I placed the flower on the table and blew out the flame and placed it next to the flower with shaking hands. I knew that my face was very pink. I did not care. The Viceroy's loving voice calmed me considerably. I said my sacred vow to the angel who represented the Emperor. He was fully twice my height so I really had to look up. His eyes were piercing but kind. I had never seen such an angel in my life; I don't believe that any mortal has.

The plan was for the angel to indicate an answer from the Emperor and I would retire to a secret cave on Patmos where the Viceroy had prayed to the Emperor for many years while he was imprisoned as a mortal there. There, for a week, I would contemplate on the Emperor and ask for a visitation from The Presence. After I finished my vow, the great angel nodded the Emperor's acceptance and immediately a portal opened just behind the angel. He leaned down and grasped me by the waist with both his mighty hands and took one quick giant step backwards. Everyone mortal and Immortal at the Dais gasped except the Viceroy. I found myself, not before, but beside the throne in Jerusalem looking into His eyes. He arose and took me by the hand and we walked away from the throne into a room on the mortal side of the throne – there was another side, an Immortal side behind the throne, I could see into it – as thousands of angels and Immortals moved aside to show the path. Inside this room with the Emperor I experienced something like a new birth. I knew that I would never be the same again. He held me and I was somehow transformed. It was all very pure and peaceful and wonderful. It seemed like it lasted just a few minutes. I had been actually gone an entire day. When I emerged by myself, I was dressed in the habit with my ring and my necklace. Either they were the very ones that were laying on a white silk pillow next to the Viceroy at Patmos or they were exact duplicates.

I learned when I returned that when the angel took me, the ring and necklace on Patmos disappeared. The necklace has a beautiful translucent white stone set inside the golden sunburst pendant, this was unexpected. They were my wedding gifts from the Emperor and I soon discovered that they were more than jewelry. As long as the ring is on my finger, I am blessed with The Presence continually. The peace is indescribable. Lucius, dear Lucius, will not touch the necklace or the ring. Only I can remove the necklace and put it back on. At first I would not remove it to bathe, but later I would take it off briefly to bathe. The ring never comes off. I also found that when I am confused about any decision, I can ask if I should go this way or that and the white stone in the sunburst pendant on the necklace will glow to indicate "Yes." No other mortal is able to see this glow. Elaine can see it. "The Urim returns," is all that she said the first time she noticed the glow. I looked this "Urim" up in the First Testament of Anna.

[N.D.] Tomorrow is my first anniversary of my marriage to the Emperor. I wondered if He would recognize it. I actually spoke to the Presence about it and I do feel that

I had been heard and that the Presence was assuring me deep inside that the Emperor would recognize our anniversary. I wondered what it would be.

[N.D.]   When I awoke this morning my servants and staff we all quite excited. They were looking outside. I went to a window and looked out. All over the garden and grounds there were thousands of blue rimmed white orchids. They were everywhere, my wedding flower. The gardeners quickly volunteered that they had never been planted. This is not the native area for these orchids. There were no supporting plants with the blooms. There was merely a stem coming through the ground. One gardener asked permission to pull only one up and examine the unusual root system. There was a novel root system; they were actually growing plants. I was told that every square foot of the residence property was thick with these flowers and that none appeared past the boundaries of my residence. It was a beautiful sight and mortals and Immortals alike were gathering to see it. Everyone knew that this was my wedding flower and that the Emperor had sent them to honor our anniversary. Before long Elaine arrived.

"Happy anniversary, little one," she said as she came to hug me. "I see that the Emperor sent flowers."

"Yes," I said smiling and laughing. "Indeed, He did send flowers; lots of flowers."

After exactly 28 days the flowers, which looked like fresh blooms every single day, vanished overnight as if they had all been pulled up and taken away by the angels.

[N.D.]   The civil executive sent a woman to the Residence today to act as my assistant and liaison to his department. Her name is Coleen and she is quite attractive. She is just a little taller and maybe five years older than myself, slim, with beautiful black hair that hangs in ringlets just above her shoulders. She is most pleasant and polite. I, of course, have the option of refusing her but I feel that she is very attractive and capable and I want to do all that I can to cooperate with the civil executive. When she left my library after that first interview, I felt a slight pressure from the Presence but I did not take the time to examine this.

[N.D.] Coleen and I have become great friends. We often eat our mid-day meal together. She asks me questions about the Emperor and I have told her almost as much as I have told Elaine. Elaine learns nothing new about the Emperor from me, but she likes to hear my side of it all. Coleen and I talk about life and laugh a lot together. She has been a real tonic for me. I had not realized how serious I had become from my involvement in my work. One day we got to watching the antics of some squirrels outside the window that the gardener was trying to keep away from the bird feeder. They got the seed and Coleen and I ended up laughing until we sounded like two giggly girls who could not stop laughing. My cook came to see if anything was wrong. Before long Elaine complained that I do not come to see her anymore.

[N.D.] Last evening I was speaking in the city about the rewards of virtuous living to a group of about 300 mortals. I noticed several people, both men and women, whispering to each other for a long time. They did not seem to take much effort to conceal their actions. They just held their hands up and talked behind them to one another. I was a little taken back as my office usually commands more respect but I did not dwell on this.

[N.D.] My librarian, James, is one of the best any Keeper has ever had. He is a tall and slender quiet man of about 40 years. He is quite efficient and seems to anticipate my interests and needs. We work together quite a lot, usually in the evenings. Sometimes when we are finished, he stays for a while to organize things for the next day and as I leave I touch him on the shoulder and he says, "Good night, Keeper."

[N.D.] I have just experienced another incident of whispering while I was talking. This is the third time this week. This time I signaled Lucius secretly to go invisible and check on it. Later back at the residence I asked him about it.

"Did you hear them clearly?" I asked. An unnecessary question.

"Yes, Keeper."

"Then tell. Come on!"

"It is unseemly, Keeper."

"About me?"

"Yes."

"Tell. Tell it all, word for word." For Lucius this was not difficult. Angels remember everything, literally.

"They spoke of you and James."

"Me and James? My librarian?"

"Yes."

"Verbatim, Lucius." I could tell that he did not want to hurt me.

"They say that all is not pure between you."

I was shocked and looked it. I looked directly at Lucius. "I will hear it all, Lucius, word for word."

"With that innocent little baby face of hers. She is wanton. She lifts her pure white skirt for him. Married to the Emperor indeed. The little tramp. So pure and white. They are illicit lovers, James and May. She simply must have him."

I was glad that my habit covers most of me because it helped to hide my blushing. Unseemly was a mild word for their thoughts and talk. Granted, we did work a lot together and I did occasionally touch his shoulder. But not in any impure way. Why were they doing this? What was the source of it? I was hurt and angry both at once. I would not ask Lucius anymore. I would consult the Presence and the necklace. I went to my chapel. I had designed my chapel; it was my favorite place. Lucius always stayed just outside the door when I was in the chapel.

[N.D.] Questions involving the necklace always have to be phrased in a manner that will accommodate a 'yes' or 'no' answer.

"Is there a single person in my company who is responsible for these rumors?"

A distinct glow emanated from the translucent white stone set in the necklace, a definite "Yes."

"Do I know this person?"

Another "Yes."

"Is this person close to me?"

Another "Yes."

"A male?'

No response. A "no."

I was thankful, this ruled out James himself.

"A female?"

"Yes."

I named every mortal female around me except one, no responses for any of them.

I did not want to name the one remaining, it hurt too much to even think about it. I took a deep breath and asked, "Coleen?"

"Yes."

I burst into tears and cried for a long time asking the Presence to help me. After I composed myself, I had two more questions.

"Was this her intent from the beginning?"

"Yes." I found that I still had some more tears. I thought I was dry.

"Was she put up to it by others?"

"Yes." That helped ease my pain a little but not much. I planned my actions on this for a couple of days before I went to Elaine. I was embarrassed to admit that I had been so taken in.

"I am sorry, little one," Elaine said. "But I had to let you learn this one on your own. I am so sorry for your pain." She held me while I cried some more. Thank the Emperor for Elaine. She was not capable of betrayal and she does love me so as I do her.

[N.D.] I had decided to keep things normal for a few weeks and Elaine agreed with my plan. I tried to hid my hurt around Coleen, but I could not bring myself to laugh with her. I was broken hearted. I hid behind my busy schedule. Sometimes I thought, I am the Keeper. I can send her packing. I can turn her over for judgment. Then I would calm down and return to my plan. I wanted her to admit to me what she had done. I could not forget the accusation that I "lifted my pure white skirt" for James. How ugly and hateful! But most of all, it was the pain of the betrayal. That Coleen had actually reported these lies. What would my Beloved do? What had he done when he was betrayed and rejected and tortured and killed? He forgave them. I had no choice. I must follow in His footsteps. It took me three days but I completely forgave her. I felt much lighter and I felt the pleasure of the Presence and therefore of my Beloved as well. But this brought a new kind of pain. I hurt for Coleen. She was carrying the guilt of this and she knew it. I waited for her to confess while I hurt for her. I realized that there had been more personal safety for me in my anger than in my forgiveness. In forgiveness I was exposed and in pain for her.

[N.D.] Eventually Coleen could stand it no longer. We were going over a publication for release when she suddenly choked up and would only look down in shame. I bent down and looked up into her eyes. They were brimming with tears. I waited. She sniffed and broke into sobs.

"Oh, May, I am so sorry! Please, Keeper, please forgive me. And, and . . . turn me over to the Metropolitan for judgment and punishment. I am a horrible person. I betrayed you with terrible lies." Sobs racked her body. I took her into my arms.

"No, no dear Coleen. I do not judge you. I forgive you. I folded her into my arms as far as I could and we both cried together. However, I thought, as for those who put you up to this, I will tell Elaine and have them arrested. When I did, Coleen rushed to bear witness against them.

[N.D.] "What were you thinking?" the Metropolitan asked.

"No one can be that good," the assistant executive responded.

"But, she is indeed," the Metropolitan said. "Sometimes I wish we had prisons," the Metropolitan remarked to his court. "But the Emperor knows best." He turned to the accused. "I could punish you for high treason, the Keeper is married to the Emperor as we Immortals are. The sentence for that is death." The man cringed. "But instead, mister executive, you will clean the streets."

"For how long, Excellency?" the man wheezed.

"Forever. Get him out of here. Wait, first, Keeper do you have anything to say?" He turned to me.

"No, Excellency. For myself I forgive him. But the Emperor's name has also been slandered."

"Fine," the Metropolitan said and gestured to some angels. The man was taken away.

[N.D.] After that Coleen was my best friend after the Emperor and Elaine. I put her on my own staff and she is very devoted. Everywhere I speak Coleen is with me.

Afterwards she will go out among the crowd and tell of her love for me and the Emperor and how she was forgiven. She is a bright jewel now.

[N.D.] Lucius woke me at 3 A.M.

"Keeper, Keeper, . . . Mistress."

He had never called me "Mistress" before. It was an honor that I did not notice at the time.

"Wha . . ., what is it, Lucius?"

"Keeper, Coleen has been badly beaten."

I jumped into my habit and necklace. "Where?"

"At the Dias."

"Now."

Elaine had the night court. It was a beautiful moonlit night. Coleen had been brought by the angels and her broken bleeding body way lying on the Dais. I knelt over her, my hands poised over her but I did not know what to do. I turned and gestured to Elaine.

"Please," I said. "Restore her, Elaine."

"You are also a bride of the Emperor, May. You have the Presence and the Urim. You do it. Really, you can."

I touched Coleen's body lightly.

"That's right. You must touch every injured area. She is badly broken. Begin at her head and touch her slowly until you get to her feet. Go slowly, let the Presence guide you and flow through you. I felt the Presence surge through my hands. I kept them still until the surging stopped, then I moved on. She started breathing. I continued. I could feel her flesh moving, sometimes reforming under my hands. In a few minutes she opened her eyes. I helped her sit up. I kept touching her. I held her. In a few more minutes she could stand. My dear Coleen.

[N.D.] The angels delivered Coleen's tormentors to the Dais. Metropolitan Henry was there. They were a part of the condemned assistant executive's group. The Metropolitan executed them on the spot, recalled the assistant executive from his street cleaning work and executed him as well for complicity in Coleen's death.

[N.D.]   My homes for children have multiplied throughout the earth. I was determined to provide a loving home for every abandoned or abused or even unappreciated child in the world. All the Immortal Princes of the earth are in full support of my project. Angels seek out children who are hurt or unwanted in any way. If there is one loving and caring parent, the children are not taken away from them. If this parent needs help in supporting or caring for the child or children, they are helped to do so. Otherwise, the children are removed or rescued and placed in one of my homes. Here I see to it that they have everything that they need. After they are reestablished and healed, they are available for adoption by worthy mortals. If they are not adopted, they grow up in the home which is well staffed with loving mortals and protected by an Immortal volunteer and angels. The angels rotate in their shifts and are under Michael's command. I visit all of the homes and hold every child. I have created an order of devoted persons to serve as child carers. They can be either female or male. I do not require them to take my vows, but they must be pure in all of their motives and actions with the children. The children are known as the Emperor's children. By His own command, officially, they are wards of the Emperor Himself. After only a few years now many of them have shown exceptional promise in many areas. The homes are never referred to as 'orphanages;' they are houses of honor not rejection.

[N.D.]   Sometimes, when I am at a Dais, I am emboldened by the Presence of the ring to intervene for those being judged. No other Keeper has ever done this. I have never been rebuked and sometimes I actually influence the judgment. On the first such occasion a scraggily young man was brought to the Dais for thievery. The Immortal Prince Carol was in charge. I do not know where the Metropolitan was, but Carol's word would be absolute. She heard all the evidence against this man. He had stolen from everybody he knew and a lot of people that he did not know. An honorable job had never entered his mind. He was a pathetic example of a human being and a man. He had abused his body in many ways, his hair was filthy and of various lengths. It looked to be dark hair but he could have been blonde; it was that dirty. He had a beard that was just as bad looking. He was very thin and he stank. When everything became quiet, Carol paused and then turned to pick up her scepter.

"Excellency," I heard myself say.

She turned to me. "Keeper May. You have something to say?"

"Yes, Excellency. I would like to, er . . .adopt him. Yes, I would like to adopt this man and try to reform him." I caught my breath. I was somewhat older than him and I was the Keeper.

"I guess that adoption principles could be interpreted that way," Carol said. She rested her chin on her scepter and thought for a while. I had presented an under governor with a novel concept. I thought it was my only hope to save the man. Finally she said, "Granted, Keeper. It is your responsibility. I would advise, however, that you have your angel watch him very closely, especially at first." She motioned to her angels and they released the man. Now it was my responsibility. I motioned to Lucius.

"Restrain him, Lucius, and take him to the Residence. Put him in the empty garden house and stay with him until I return."

"Keeper, yourself . . ."

"I will be fine. Carol will loan me an escort." I glanced at Carol. She nodded.

After Lucius left, Carol wanted to talk. Of course, it was fine with me.

"May, I've been wanting to ask you why you wanted to restore a monastic lifestyle."

"Oh, well, I guess you could say that I just stumbled on the concept in my reading. Then I asked Janice about it, she was a nun, you know."

Carol nodded. There was no business at the Dais now and there were not many people there. I continued.

"And I love the Emperor. I can not help myself; I just love Him. So I petitioned to be married to him after the monastic manner and, well, it was granted."

"You don't mind the sacrifice, I mean what you had to give up as a mortal to do this," Carol asked.

"No, not at all. My love for Him overshadows everything else. I mean, I have human needs, but I chose this way and I am so blessed and honored that I was accepted."

"I know about the needs," Carol said. "I was a married woman as a mortal. I had a good marriage. My husband, my former husband, is here and two of our children."

"You liked family life then?"

"Oh yes, I can still remember the sweetness of it. My husband and I always had a good love life and later when the children came it was good. I remember those mornings when they would all pile into bed with us and we would tumble and play with them. They were so warm and sweet. I loved being a wife and a mother. I don't know whether as a mortal I could have chosen to give that up."

"Well, you didn't have to. You were believers."

"True. I was just wondering how you bear it."

"Sometimes, I am lonely and hungry for things I can not have," I replied. "But it is worth it. May I ask you something?"

"Of course."

"What is it like now. You are no longer married as an Immortal. Surely there is nothing that you miss."

"You're right. Jerry and I are still close as Immortals. We will always be. And our children, two of them are here, the third one didn't make it. He was the middle child and always rebellious. That is still painful, but our fellowship with the other Immortals and the Emperor overshadows our pain. Our oldest is a Metropolitan; he excelled for the Emperor and the youngest and her entire mortal family are here. You see, what we have in fellowship with each other and the Emperor is a closeness that we could never know as mortals. It is not the same kind of physical closeness that we had in marriage. We now have new bodies, but they are different. It is hard to explain. I could not have understood it as a mortal. But this closeness is all consuming and complete. It is not completely spiritual; we do feel it with our physical selves, but it is not like a mortal feeling or desire."

"You're right. I can not really understand. But I can accept it," I said.

"May, you are a wonder."

"Thanks. I love you Carol."

"And I love you." We hugged. One of the Dais angels took me back to my residence.

When I got home, I ordered my newfound ward to shave and bathe. I touched his chest and asked the Presence to release him from his various addictions. He was very surprised when he felt this happen. I found out his name was Lee. He responded well to care and instruction. Within a few months he was unrecognizable from his former state. He showed an interest in gardening and my gardener trained him. He is a good gardener and he is always grateful. The Metropolitan says that I did a good job with Lee. I have decided to recruit other loyal and descent subjects to adopt such men and women. I have called this work the Redemption Society and dedicated it to the Emperor. Its work is coordinated with my Children's Society.

[N.D.] Once a year, in the spring, most all of the Immortals disappear for 3 days. There are still enough to dominate every Dais, one or maybe two of them. Even then they only serve in four 6 hour shifts and are then relieved by some other Immortals. A normal number of angels remain during this time. No one has ever asked why this is. I could not contain my curiosity. I dropped by at Elaine's residence two days before this strange absence was to begin. My librarian had detailed records of these absences for the past 30 years. No one knows why he kept them, but I could see a plain pattern.

[N.D.] "Elaine," I called as soon as Lucius and I were clear of the portal.
"Here," she answered from her garden. Lucius had placed me within five feet of her. I went to the garden.
"May, dear, look at these," she said. I went over to inspect the basket of flowers that she had picked. They were all beautiful. Elaine loved her garden and her flowers.
"They are beautiful," I said.
"Yes, they surely are." She admired them for a while and arranged them partially in the basket.
"Elaine?"
"I always know when a question is coming from you, dear," she said.
I smiled. "And you know what it is also, I suppose?" Even Lucius had told me once that I was the first Keeper to treat Elaine so familiarly. That was fine with me.

"Yes, I do, smarty," she said as she lightly pinched my check.

I really felt like we were sisters. One Immortal and one mortal, for now.

"Yes, it is only two days now."

"Uh-huh."

She sat down next to her basket and I joined her.

"We celebrate a very special time with the Emperor, there is constant banqueting for the entire three days."

I waited. I would not interrupt a word.

"We celebrate that horrible and wonderful act when the Emperor overcame death for us all. May, dearest, I would have told you about it sooner, but I did not want to hurt you because you can't go with us. I knew you would want to." She touched my cheek softly and looked into my eyes.

"I do not expect to go beyond the veil with you, I know that my body can not. And it is enough that I have experienced His embrace and have the Presence with me. I am greatly honored."

"I should have known. You are very mature."

"Something that you did not know," I teased.

"Yes, sometimes my emotions can get in my way."

"I see your Immortality so clearly, that I forget your humanity," I said.

"That is understandable," she responded.

"But, but . . . this year, dear one, I have arranged a little something special for you."

"Tell."

"Well." She pulled her legs under her and sat up very straight. "This year you will lead a banquet at the Temple in Jerusalem for twenty three special mortals from around the world, twenty four including yourself."

I was excited and still in need of more information.

She continued. "On the second day while we are banqueting beyond the veil you twenty four will be banqueting on your side. The Presence will communicate to you the Emperor's Words. The other twenty three, some of them you know, some you have awarded yourself, are singled out for outstanding loyalty to the Emperor and work in your Children's and Redemption Societies. You will be the hostess."

I could hardly tend to my duties while I waited for the day. Lucius took me and other angels were assigned temporarily to the other twenty-three mortals. It was a wonderful banquet and the Words of the Emperor were wonderful; however, they will not be recorded even in my private journals. Sorry.

Elaine tells me that this will be an annual event as long as I am the Keeper. This first banquet occurred in the 9th year of my office.

[N.D.]   My tenth wedding anniversary was wonderfully unique. As usual, everyone was expecting the orchids to appear. So I arose with the sun that morning and, as expected, the orchids were everywhere on the grounds of the Residence. As I wanted to have my breakfast, I always dressed completely as soon as I arose, I turned to see not only Lucius but that mighty angel that had taken me to the Emperor on the day that I was married. He nodded. I nodded. I waited. The Presence did not prod me to do anything, so I continued to wait. I decided to stand my ground as long as the angel did. For some reason there were no servants or staff anywhere near by. I stood with my back to the window and stared at this great angel. There were certainly no others like him to be seen anywhere on the earth. I was in my formal reception room which is quite large. Lucius and the great angel were blocking the doorway opposite. Two other angels exactly like the great one appeared and blocked the other two doors on either side. Then a sort of screen seemed to emanate from all three of them which obscured all three doorways. Then all four of them, Lucius included, turned around so that I saw only their backs. I felt someone behind me between me and the window different than the Presence. I gasped with joy. He put His arms around me and I almost passed out. He whispered in my ear what a wonderful job I was doing and some love words that I will not record. Then he released me and I turned to look at His face and to get lost once again in His eyes. Again, time passed in the room but not in my heart or mind. I had no idea how long He had been there when He departed. The great angels left with Him, only Lucius remained. There was no other escort this time. Lucius was facing me now.

"How, how long, Lucius?" I asked.

"It is dinner time, Keeper," he responded.

"Has anyone been to see me?"

"No, Keeper, no one has come. I would have turned them away while His Majesty was here."

I was not hungry, I went to bed and slept the night through.

[N.D.] In an effort to represent my offices everywhere, I will make a continual tour of many Principalities each year. When I presented my proposed annual agenda through Lucius to the Emperor, I was told that it would be communicated to every Dais and, in addition, I would no longer need permission to visit any Dais at any time. This is a great honor that I will not abuse.

[N.D.] My schedule is roughly as follows. From my home at the Dais of the Metropolitan Henry Sawyer I circle the world working East and Northward for the first half of the year. During the second half I repeat this pattern working West and towards the South. My first stop of the year is Lisbon.

[N.D.]   The Metropolitan of Lisbon is Jorge
Romero. He is one of my favorites. Jorge always makes me
laugh. He is not only joyful, he is funny. Before I met him,
I did not believe that any Metropolitan, or even any
Immortal, could be as funny as he is. He is not tall for a
man, he has dark skin and hair and eyes. His eyes always
twinkle. Part of that are the tiny wrinkles in the corners of
his eyes, but mostly it is the actual twinkle in his eyes. He
is funny but never at the expense of others; he does not say
or do anything that demeans or insults any individual
mortal or Immortal. He does joke about himself a lot and he
will tease, but somehow it is never demeaning. When I first
met him, he said, "Please call me Jorge, may I call you
May, May?" I responded, "Certainly Jorge," and he said,
"great May May." So now I am usually "May May" to him.
Sometimes I will visit his Dais just for the joy of it. This
visit, however, was the first on my present tour and the way
I have set it up, it will always be the first. When I arrived,
he stopped what he was doing and walked directly towards
me and hugged me.

"Oh, welcome, May May, you have been far too
long from my Dais."

"Jorge, it is so good to see you."

"This fellow," he said pointing to the mortal before
him, "this fellow has invented the most unbelievable
scheme to steal from his employer and the government that
I have ever seen. I am not sure I understand it yet."

The accused looked shamefully at the ground.

Jorge turned to one of his under governors, "Do you
understand it, Paolo?"

"No, Excellency, not exactly. It has something to do
with relabeling the product and only giving the mortal
executive one item instead of a pair of the same number,
then reselling the other half to a competitor at a higher
price who in turn sells them to the executive, as well, under
another name."

"Yes, something like that," Jorge said. "The witnesses against him are reputable and he has admitted to it all. You know, Keeper, if his kind would expend the same amount of energy and ingenuity doing honest work, they could do so much for everyone."

I nodded in agreement. Jorge motioned for me to take a seat. He paused then turned towards the accused and walked slowly towards him. "So, my friend, do you have anything else to say for yourself?"

The man stood silent.

"Here comes the judge," Jorge said.

The man flinched.

Jorge looked at his scepter lying on the small table next to his chair, then he looked at me, then at the accused, then back at me and winked. I tried not to smile. Then I had a thought. Each Immortal ruler has his or her own style and I was catching on to Jorge's.

"I could use him in my work," I said.

"You could?"

"Yes, such a ingenious and inventive man would be a lot of help."

Jorge smiled, "Then he is yours, Keeper."

The man looked perplexed and suspicious at the same time.

In my mind I asked the Presence for quick wisdom and creativity. Then it came to me.

"What is your name?' I asked the man.

"Giovanni, Keeper."

"Like the Viceroy?" I asked.

"Yes, Keeper."

"How could you disgrace such a name?" I asked.

"I do not know. I am ashamed."

"Then I will give you a chance to make amends. You know that you must pay back all of what you have stolen?"

He gulped.

"Yes, you will work for me. You will be paid in gold, of which you will be allowed to keep one fifth for your needs until all is restored. Your pay will not be high. Do you understand?"

"Yes, I understand." He did not look happy.

I paused.

"And you shall earn this by entertaining my children."

"Your children?"

"Yes, the children in my homes, the Emperor's children."

"How? How can I do this?" Giovanni asked.

"I am sure that you can find a way. Remember, you must make them laugh and you must be kind to them always."

"I like children, Keeper. I will be kind. But, I am not sure that I can make them laugh as you wish."

"You will find a way. You will not be punished if you can not make them laugh. But if you ever hurt one, I will have you sent right back here. Do you understand?"

He nodded.

"And," the Metropolitan said, "If you come before me again . . ." He picked up his scepter and pointed the sharp end directly at Giovanni.

Giovanni showed stark fear.

"About this I have no humor," Jorge stated firmly. "Hold him for the Keeper's instructions."

I visited with Jorge for a long time. It was a grand start for my tour. Just before I went to bed in the beautiful room that Jorge provided for me, Lucius interrupted, "Keeper, what about this man, Giovanni?"

"Oh, I am sorry, Lucius. Send him to my home supervisor – how many languages does he speak?"

"His own and the universal, Keeper."

"Then send him to the supervisor in Atlanta so Elaine can help me watch him. Be sure that what I said on the Dais is communicated clearly. He will work out fine and the children will help change him. He has a soft heart and they will love him."

"Yes, Keeper."

[N.D.] On my nineteenth anniversary the Viceroys declared that I would also carry the title of Spiritual Primate of all the mortals of the earth and that this title would pass to my successors. I have added a crest to Mark's robe which passes to each Keeper. Since I took my habit, I no longer wear the robe on any occasion. The crest is a simple bronze shield about five inches in height with a white open book in the center and the word "truth" under the book.

[N.D.] I love to visit the Viceroy John because he will talk to me for hours about his friendship with the Emperor. There is no lack of respect for the Emperor's majesty or power in the Viceroy's heart or soul. Perhaps more than any Immortal John knows the Emperor. He is totally aware of the Emperor's blinding glory, but, at the same time, he is intimately aware of His humanity. The Viceroy's Dais is one that I visit more frequently in the great privilege given me by the Emperor to visit any Dais at any time without an appointment. At Patmos I always direct Lucius to bring me into the pavilion behind the Dais so I can enter quietly from the side. John will notice me almost immediately and smile even if he can not stop what he is doing at the time. I will get myself a drink at the pavilion and sit down at the end of the highest row of the Dais and wait. This day John was addressing an angel Prince.

"Please be sure to check with Raphael to be certain where the Emperor wants to begin with this," the Viceroy was saying.

The great angel nodded.

The Viceroy waived his hand to dismiss him and the great angel was gone.

"May, hello, you have been missed."

I scurried over and kissed his hand. He put his finger under my chin to turn my face up and looked into my eyes. I returned his gaze scarcely blinking to soak up the love.

"Dear May, if you stay away so long again I shall have to punish you," he smiled. I was not frightened. Even if he did rule half the earth. He continued looking into my eyes. "I can not find a speck of impurity."

"Excellency, I am not so pure," I protested.

The Viceroy turned to a beautiful Immortal man with red hair and said, "David, come and see, our little Keeper is such a dear."

This Immortal approached and looked into my eyes. I had not met this man before. As far as I knew, he was not a Metropolitan or an Over-Lord.

"May," The Viceroy's voice seemed distant. "David is the Chancellor of the Imperial Court. After the Emperor we all defer to him."

I heard the words but I did not understand.

"She has the same spirit as my third wife," David said.

"Abigail, yes. I would like her to meet May."

I was still staring at the Chancellor when I suddenly understood. I am ashamed at being so slow. At least I did not display my ignorance. I have read the First Testament of Anna.

"Excellency, it is such an honor," I said to the now Immortal ancient King of Israel.

"And I have heard of May, the only mortal wife of His Majesty," David said. He turned to an angel. "Ask the Lady Abigail to please join us, " he said. The angel vanished.

I talked for hours with the Lady Abigail. We talked of many things over at the side of the Dais. She is delightful. A beautiful Immortal. We talked of her mortality and of mine, of how they are the same in some respects and different in others. I have had a burning question on my heart for some time and I felt that she was identifying with my mortality, perhaps even more than Elaine does, since Elaine's mortality was in a more privileged time than mine or Abigail's. I decided to venture some questions.

"Abigail?"

"May."

"When you were mortal, . . . did you know for sure that you would get an Immortal life and body? You see, Elaine, my governor and friend, was sure. But I am not. Not totally."

"We were not as sure as Elaine. But the teaching was known among us. I became sure because David was sure."

"He   was?"

"Yes, always, with never a doubt."

"How?"

"The same way, dear May," she took my hand in hers. She had very feminine hands but mine were lost in hers. "The same way that David did. Because he knew the Emperor. He really knew Him."

I was quiet.

"May," she continued, "you really know deep in your heart that you are immortal. The Emperor will raise you up and give you an immortal body. Just commune in your heart and you will know. Ask the Presence to help."

"In your day did you have the Presence as I do?"

"Yes, He came to us and was upon us, especially upon leaders. In Elaine's day he indwelt them. Now He is upon you as in my day. But you have also been held by the Emperor."

I blushed.

"Dear child," She tightened her grip. "so you know, you really do."

I nodded. The most important thing in all of life and I was so choked up all I could do was nod.

"We are held by Him frequently on the other side. But you are the only mortal now who has been held by Him. You are sure. You will be fine."

I was sure. And being sure I was then able to ask for others. "What about other mortals now?" I asked.

"What do you think?"

"I think I will encourage them all to trust Him," was my answer.

Abigail smiled.

"What was your transformation like? I have talked to Elaine."

"We were bodiless in a shadowy place. When the Emperor finished his wonderful redeeming sacrifice, He came to us and led us out."

"Where did he lead you?"

"To our new homes that He had prepared for us."

About this time the Chancellor returned.

"Jonathan, my brother, I am returning to the Mansion, do you want to return with me." Another Immortal man appeared.

"Yes, David, I am ready."

"Abigail?"

"Yes, I will come now."

The Chancellor turned to me. "You have leave to attend any place you desire?"

"Yes, Excellency. Everywhere except the capital."

He turned to Lucius. "You are the Keeper's angel."

"Yes, Excellency."

"From now on she can come to the capital including the Throne room at will."

"Yes, Excellency."

108

I was wild with joy. This meant that I could see the Emperor any time I wanted to.

"Thank you, Excellency," I said beaming with tears in my eyes.

All he did was smile. As he passed by me, he gave me a hug and kissed me on the top of my head. As he came to Abigail and Jonathan, he raised his hand and they were gone.

[N.D.] I was so excited. I tried to decide when I would go to the capital first. I waited for a couple of days and then I could stand it no longer. I turned to Lucius. "The Throne Room, please, Lucius." He obeyed and we were there. I was still a little surprised as it was almost too wonderful to believe. But the Chancellor was the Chancellor. Lucius deposited me on one side of the Throne. The Emperor was awarding some fortunate mortals praise for their work in a once-in-a-lifetime ceremony. He glanced my way and smiled. I had to sit down as I got weak in the knees when He smiled at me. I was afraid that this was a breach in protocol, but no one seemed to mind and John looked at me and smiled so I did not try to get up. After He was done, the Emperor turned to pass through the veil and walked by me first and hugged me and gave me a kiss on the top of my head. I sat down again. This is wonderful.

[N.D.] I made a mistake on my second visit to the Throne because I did not give myself enough time. I tried to fit it into a fairly busy schedule. When I arrived, the Emperor was not there and I started to leave. The Chancellor was talking to some Immortals beside the Throne and saw me. He motioned for me to stay, I presumed that he knew that the Emperor would arrive soon and I was right. Before long He arrived and smiled at me on his way to the Throne. Several awards were being given that day. Before long I realized that I was about to be late for my appointment with Viceroy Cepata. I did not know what to do. Slowly I rose. He saw me and waved. I was free to leave. In the future I will allow myself more time. If the Emperor is not there and I am not bid to stay by the Chancellor or a Viceroy, then I can simply leave and come back later.

[N.D.] Today the Emperor was not there when I arrived. I had plenty of time so I studied the veil and tried to see beyond it and thought of the wonder of the capital. The entire capital is surrounded by many Legions of angels. They form a canopy over and around the city. The city is unbelievably beautiful with many fountains and green bushes and many colored flowers everywhere. The fountains produce an almost continuous sound as you are never far from one and often within hearing distance of two or three. The temple dominates the city from the temple mound. It glistens. The palace is next to the temple and is equally beautiful. Both have enormous golden doors which always stand open. A light emanates from the temple-palace area. Although it is always a beautiful sky, the light from this area is stronger than the sun except that it does not hurt the eyes. Many of the population of the city are Immortal. Some of the mortals are visiting administrators and other prominent people in the kingdom.

The throne room is in the Temple and is beyond description. It is enormous and filled with light. There are some very special angels in the throne room. They are larger and brighter and more beautiful than any angels that I have seen in other places on earth. The throne sits in the middle of a marble-like Dais which really shines. There are twelve steps up to the throne and there are no other seats on the Dais. A wide permanent sort of portal is always open behind the throne. You can not see very far in because of a sort of mist or veil. But if you stand to the side of the audience chamber you can tell that there is another throne back to back to the one here, or perhaps they have a common back, one throne with a seat on each side. There was a light sweet smelling mist inside the room. No discipline cases are brought before the Emperor. The sweetness and the peace of the place was addictive.

[N.D.] Not only do I have the pleasure of being in with the Emperor in the Throne room, but there are Immortals there that we mortals do not see anywhere else. I realize that there are millions of Immortals on the other side of the veil. Some of them may never come to this side. As I was waiting on the Emperor to appear one day, a few Immortals were meeting with the Chancellor beside the Throne. I could hear that they were talking about some places that they called Imperial Parklands. At first I presumed that these were the parks that surrounded most of the Dais' in the world. But I did not recognize any of the names that I was hearing. It soon became clear to me that there were enormous reserves that have been set aside for the Immortals to enjoy if they want to be near the beauties of nature. Of course, now these places are not so harsh and dangerous as they were during their mortality. When he was done with his meeting, the Chancellor came towards me.

"May."

"Excellency." I bowed slightly.

"He will not be here today at all, little one." There was so much love in his voice that I did not even notice being called "little one."

"Thank you, Chancellor. Perhaps I will return to my duties and come back another day."

"You overheard about the parklands?"

"Yes, Excellency."

"You may visit them, your know. Your angel will take you."

"That would be wonderful."

"Make the rounds and find the ones that you like best. You will also meet some interesting Immortals."

I did not know which would be the most interesting, the Parklands or the Immortals. The Chancellor grasped me tenderly by the shoulders and kissed the top of my head again and walked through the veil.

"Lucius."

The first place that Lucius took me was called "The Mara." It was on the African continent near the Southeast coast. It is very beautiful. There are beautiful green parklands and many beautiful animals. There are thousands of families of lions and the Immortals romp and play with them and the other animals. The antelopes are all mixed in with the lions and there are lots of wonderful fruits for them both to eat. There were many Immortals present; they pop in and out of here directly from the Mansion. Some of them are rulers, but most of them are not. There are many mortal caretakers and a few angels. My habit makes me stand out, but I can not change it for other clothing because of my vows. I saw a large group of Immortals picnicking under a clump of trees so I walked in that direction. I did not want to impose myself on them so I did not go directly into their group. One of them motioned for me to come closer and they smiled and offered me some fruit. Several motioned for me to sit down. They were clustered around a woman in the center. Her face showed that she had died as a mature, older woman. Before long she looked at me and said, " I see that the young Keeper, May, has joined us. Welcome child."

"Thank you, Ma'am." I did not know what else to say.

"Come here, child," she said as she patted a patch of grass next to her.

I obeyed quickly.

She put her arm around me and kissed the top of my head. They all seem to like to kiss me on the head. She is a very sweet woman.

"You don't know who I am, do you?"

"No Ma'am."

"My name is Mary."

"The Emperor's mother!" I almost shouted. I was so embarrassed. They all laughed good naturedly.

"Yes." she smiled. "You might say that I am your mother-in-law."

They laughed softly again.

"Don't be frightened, child. No one is frightened of me," she said.

"Yes Ma'am."

"Here, you can meet some more of the family." She waived to some men in the distance and shouted, "James, Jude, Joseph, come here."

Three men ran over.

"Yes, mother," they said practically in unison.

"This is the little Keeper, May. Give her a nice welcome. These three Immortal men, the Emperor's brothers, greeted me warmly, and as usual, kissed the top of my head. I would have to get used to this. I felt like family. And I am still but a mortal. I could hardly believe that I wasn't dreaming. What had the Chancellor said? "You will also meet some interesting Immortals?" Interesting was hardly the word for it.

[N.D.] Against my own policy I slipped away from the Dais of the Metropolitan of Damascus where I had been discussing my children's home to see if I could catch the Emperor in the Throne room. I am well aware that Lucius could tell me this but I would much rather just drop in. He was not there when I arrived but John was. It was usually a toss up whether he would be at his Dais or in the Throne

Room or beyond the veil. He came over to me shortly after I arrived.

"Excellency." I greeted him first.

"May, I am glad you are here today. Someone special will be here soon with the Emperor. He is the Master Of The Feast." My eyes widened, a new person and a new position for me. "When we feast with the Emperor behind the veil, he is in charge. It is a wonderful place that he has," Chancellor David continued. I thought that if the Chancellor thinks it is such a wonderful place that this man has, and he is the Chancellor of the Imperial Court, then this must indeed be a special Immortal. About then the Emperor stepped through the veil almost before Michael could announce Him with another man. The Chancellor took me by the arm and fairly dragged me over to the Throne. I knelt before my Love and He embraced me briefly. The Chancellor kept me from getting too giddy and pulled me up to meet this other man. The Emperor did not seem to mind.

"Peter, this is our May."

I did not have to be told who Peter way. I know the Second Testament well enough. "Sir," I said, "Excellency, I . . ."

Peter touched my hands which I had clasped to my chest and said, "I am but a fisherman, child. Don't be too impressed. King David here is our Chancellor, be impressed with him." He smiled.

The Chancellor smiled and looked back at Peter. "You always enjoy teasing me, don't you, brother?"

"Only because I love you, sire."

"There is only one 'sire' around here, Peter, and we all know it right well," David responded.

"Grandfather." The Emperor said firmly. Peter looked at David and raised his eyebrows.

"Simon." Peter lowered his brows.

"If you two keep at it, I will send you both back to the Mansion," the Emperor interrupted. He was smiling and they both knew it.

"Yes, Master," they chimed in unison.

Never have I witnessed such a casual display of affection between the Emperor and anyone, not to mention between the Emperor, the Chancellor and the Master Of The Feast. After this the Emperor held out his hand to me. I kissed it impulsively and to my great joy He kissed mine in return. David motioned for me to resume my seat to the side. I watched some fortunate mortals receive some awards and then quietly backed away. The Emperor looked at me and smiled and I had leave to go. I was beside myself with joy for several days. Lucius seemed amused.

[N.D.] Each year I get reports that all of my various projects throughout the world are thriving. I am very happy about this. I never tire of being on a Dais when some poor soul is being tried for some disobedience. I believe that I still manage to lessen the sentence of quite a few although I sometimes suspect that the ruler involved makes a place for my participation. What a wonderful life.

03.03.358 C.R. My name is Orin, I am the nephew of May. The year is 358 C.R. Aunt May died early this morning on the 20th anniversary of her vows to the Emperor. She was only 38 but she was not sick, she had never been sick. Millions of blue bordered white orchids appeared throughout the earth as they had appeared at her Residence on each anniversary. She had done innumerable acts of mercy throughout the world. She had intervened in many judgments at many Dais' and had actually caused many judgments to be reduced. Many healings and miracles are attributed to her. No other Keeper has ever done such things. There was a massive memorial honoring her at every Dais in the world. Aunt May has affirmed for years that she believed that she would appear before the Emperor in an Immortal body and live with Him forever although she did not know when this would happen. She has given us all hope. The same mighty angel who represented the Emperor at her marriage arrived and retrieved the sunburst necklace and ring. In a few minutes he returned again and indicated that he was going to take her body as well. We all said our "goodbyes" and he picked up her body tenderly and was gone. None of us saw a portal open.

4 * JOAN

639 - 699 C.R.

02.19.639 C.R. My name is Joan. I am the daughter of Andrew, the eighth heir to Mother Anna. My father's work has been monumental and he completed the timeline of the pre-reign era and filled in many unknown and dark sections. I am now 18 years of age and my dear father Andrew has died. He has prepared me since childhood to succeed him. Elaine has given me permission to continue the work and the angel Lucius is now constantly with me. My mother, Alicia, is still mourning as I am but she is very proud of my succession.

[N.D.] I am happy to include in my journal the following from my father's.
My name is Andrew, son of Patricia and father of Joan. My wife Alicia and I have been very excited about the birth of our baby. We are old to be first time parents. I have always been busy as the successor to Mother Anna and I have specialized on the era just about two hundred years prior to the Glorious Return of the Emperor. It was a very interesting period especially since the Emperor's people during that time did not really know how long it would be before the great event. Many different groups claimed to know the time of the return, but these times would come and pass and still no return. Many began to doubt that it would ever happen. So many records were destroyed during the wars prior to the present Reign that it is a slow and painful task to piece together history between the first and second appearances. Mother Anna had started with the religious era after the Emperor left this world. She

had taken things up to the era of the dark times. My predecessors in the line have each filled in some part of the history after that. Our people are reading these accounts so that they might have a better understanding of the current reign which has existed for five hundred and sixty-six years now. Our Joan is celebrating her 16th birthday today. We are so proud of her. She has been studying very hard to be worthy of being my successor. Elaine says that she is confident that Joan will be designated. When the time comes, I will feel confident leaving it all in her hands.

02.21.639 C.R. I, Joan, am the ninth in succession from Mother Anna. I was affirmed in my offices in the year 639 Christus Regnus, of the Glorious Reign of the Emperor who rules the whole earth from Jerusalem. I am the Keeper of the Ancient Books, the Primary Interpreter of the books of Anna, the Chronicler of Imperial truth, and the Spiritual Primate of the mortals on the earth. I live in the Keeper's Residence which has been here for four generations now. Some call it a palace. Occasionally some pot stirrer will become very vocal about our style of life and authority. His complaints pass through the mortal courts to the high court where the decision is reviewed by Elaine or the Metropolitan himself. The high court has always refused to allow any charges against us to stand and the Immortals have always affirmed the decision of the mortal high court. I am, however, concerned that someday the mortal high court will rule against us in some way, my father warned me about this, and Elaine will have to reverse them. This might cause some to be punished for rebellion.

I am greatly privileged to stand in the place of my ancestral grandmother, but the responsibility of the offices also weigh heavily upon me. I have asked Elaine to correct me firmly and often. She has assured me that she will not let me go astray in any way. I do love her so. I feel so young to begin these duties.

02.22.639 C.R.   My opening report: There is no concept of rampant violence or hardship in our world. The Princes keep everything, every event, even the forces of nature, in perfect steadiness. For myself and all mortals life is smooth and beautiful. We all have a pleasant life and I have a great deal of prestige in my position. The continuation of the titles to me from my father was not automatic. Elaine decided that I was the heir. I love Elaine, but most especially I want to be able to go where she goes. After she returns to us, there is a wonderful aroma about her, it is very sweet and communicates peace to myself and all the mortals. There seems to be an aroma from her breath itself, as if she breathes a different air in that place. The very air must be strongly scented and permeates everything there is. I have followed after Elaine on many occasions as she prepares to leave and longed to go with her. She will look at me as if to say that she is sorry that I can not go. Like a child I want to go where she goes. She told me once that she would like to take me, but that my body, which is somewhat different than hers, could not survive when she goes to places which are not in this world. She had hinted that I will be given some knowledge of this place. I think of it as distant but she tells me that it is actually very near.

06.12.649 C.R.   This morning the guard informed my secretary that the chief magistrate of the mortal appeals court begs an immediate audience. The civil magistrate rarely requests an audience with The Spiritual Primate outside the normal schedule so I granted it as soon as I felt myself presentable. The magistrate, Cyril LaBaise, is fully 40 years my senior in age and I always feel a little uncertain in his presence but I try to hide it. The magistrate swept himself into my presence and stretching one foot out in front of himself bowed dramatically. In doing this he made full use of his long black robes with its snow white under suit. I always had to secretly credit the magistrate for his impressive style; he was nothing if not dramatic and very swank.

"Your Excellency," he said loudly and very clearly. He glanced briefly at Lucius just behind me to my left.

"Justice LaBaise," I used his honorary title which always pleased him.

Cyril LaBaise actually smiled. What a morning.

"I have, ah, one . . . small, small but vital matter to seek your counsel on today, Excellency." He came toward me so fast that I almost backed away but I held my ground all the time telling myself that I was the Primate.

It seems that my sister's son has presumed to infringe on your authority. I approached both the Governor Elaine and Metropolitan Sawyer on his behalf and they have referred me to you. For a moment he almost looked sheepish.

"I was not aware of this," I answered.

"Yes, it seems that at a public reading of the ancient books, during a public time of sharing, he claimed to have exclusive knowledge as to the meaning of a certain passage. It is from Anna 9 verses 13 through 21.

I nodded, I knew the passage. He, nevertheless, produced his copy of the book and read the entire passage which dealt with a church high council of the Immortals when they were still themselves mortal and it pertained to the person of the Emperor Himself. In this council the Emperor, although absent at the time from the mortal realm, was declared to be "Very God of Very God."

"This boy, young Cyril Benton, my namesake I am afraid," the magistrate went on, "had the audacity to proclaim to all present, a crowd of about thirty-five or so, that he alone understands these words. That they refer to the Emperor's deity and that he Himself, Praise His Glorious name, was never truly a mortal man. I have chided him severely. He seems genuinely repentant. What would you have us do with him, Excellency?"

For once the magistrate looked truly humble in my sight. I stood up very straight and glanced over my shoulder at Lucius. The magistrate showed slight signs of visible panic. Then I spoke very slowly and clearly.

"Send this young man to me," I instructed. "He is merely lacking in proper instruction."

The magistrate looked extremely relieved. He recovered his composure and backed away. I had never experienced such deference from him. I suddenly became more aware of my powers and responsibilities and I was honored that Elaine and the Metropolitan had referred the Justice directly to me. This was my very first case as Primate and I breathed a sigh of relief after he was gone. I was looking forward to meeting young Cyril. He was probably close to my age.

06.14.649 C.R.   Young Cyril is a very interesting young man. He arrived the very afternoon after my meeting with his uncle. I told my doorman to make him comfortable in a room of his own in the residential annex and that I would have time to see him after luncheon. The doorman returned to say that Cyril did not bring a change of clothes and had returned home for his bags. After luncheon I sent for him to come to my study and he arrived immediately. He is a tall man with light hair. He is graceful and somewhat dramatic. He knocked.

"Come."

He entered and stood there.

I looked up from my books. "Please be seated."

He finally decided on a chair exactly opposite me and looked directly at me.

"Ma'am."

That sounded a bit strange. If anything, I am younger than he is.

"Please call me Joan."

"Uh, Excellency, that would not be, uh . . ."

"It's quite alright, really." I smiled. He smiled back. The ice was broken.

Cyril has a very bright and focused mind. We dealt with his heresy first and I soon convinced him from the complete versions of the Second Testament that the Emperor was and always had been both man and God. He became even more respectful of His Majesty. He expressed his desire to see the Emperor. I told him that I had not yet had the honor myself. We talked long and hard on many subjects and he was glad to have access to my library. Most of the works in the hands of the people had been summarized for them by my predecessors. We became very involved. One evening while we were sitting in my garden I allowed him to kiss me. He began to talk marriage. I knew that I would have to consult Elaine about this but I put it off. Cyril began to talk about his expectations. He wanted several children and asked if I could handle a family along with my responsibilities. I told him that I was sure that I could. I began to experience considerable mood swings. I could not sleep. I would lie awake for long periods of time wondering if I was making the right decision. Finally, I could get no peace until I decided that I must put everything into my work. When I told Cyril, he was devastated.

"My dear, I did not intend to upset you. It, it is not because you are the Keeper that I fell in love with you. I love Joan. Have I ever asked for any special favors of you in your offices?"

"No, no Cyril. You are a dear. And if I could marry, I would marry you. I am simply convinced that I must put everything into my work. I am so sorry. You are still welcome here and we can study together."

That was not enough for him. The next day we had a tearful parting. I would miss him always.

Elaine came to see me the next day.

"My dear Elaine." I ran into her arms and discovered that I was crying.

"There, dear Joan." She held me tenderly. "What is it?"

I told her my story. She was very sympathetic and kind.

"We are a lot alike, Joannie."

She had never called me that before. "Alike? I am a mortal."

"I gave my all for the Emperor's labors as well. I died a virgin. You will not regret it. You may be lonely, but in the end it will be worth it. You will have me for a friend, " she said holding my face in her hands and smiling sweetly. I have often been very glad for her friendship. She is my best friend.

[N.D] I read in my grandmother Anna's journal that things were not as peaceful when our Immortals were mortal. There was war and starvation and sickness and violence and great fear. The Emperor was in that other place with his Father. Whole nations would war against each other and people were not permitted to die in peace. The rulers were mortal themselves. There were some mortals who were committed to the Emperor and awaiting his return. But his power was not recognized by all. So they were a secret army alone in a strange land. There was also an evil prince who could not be seen by the mortals who inspired the hate and violence and misery. At the present time this evil prince is in prison elsewhere held by the Emperor's power. I am glad of that. We live in peace. The Immortals rule righteously and there is no hunger or sickness under the emperor's reign.

[N.D.] By the time that I was invested with the title of Prime Interpreter of the Sacred Writings and my other titles I had all but memorized the writings. These writings include the ancient First Testament which was given to my Great grandmother Anna by the Immortal Elaine herself. In this testament the origins of the earth are described as well as the Law of Moses, the history of the ancient kingdom and its downfall and restoration. Also, given to Anna and now in my possession is the ancient Second Testament of the Emperor when he came in among us in great humility and the activities of those who were called out to Him. Finally, there is the Third Testament of Anna which chronicles the history of the Emperor's hidden army for two millennia until the Glorious Return. The people have been given the First and Second Testaments in summary form by Anna and the Third Testament, sometimes called the Testament of the Presence, is entirely the work of Anna herself under the guidance of Elaine. Elaine leaves the interpretation of these works almost entirely to me. It seems that it is not a job for the Immortals. As the Prime Interpreter I speak in many great theaters around the world. Lucius always transports me to these events. I never remember anything about the transport. It is, no doubt, instantaneous for Lucius and for me. When a mortal is transported the opening of a portal is necessary; the Immortals and angels do not require a portal; they are simply found to be in another place.

04.12.652 C.R.   I recently read Anna's account of her visit to the Viceroy's court at Patmos Island. I have been there several times and it is always as beautiful as she described it and John, the Viceroy, is wonderful. I asked Elaine about two other close friends of the Emperor, Peter and James. Neither of them has a court or a dominion on this earth.

"Well, I can't tell you too many specifics," Elaine answered me. "But, of course, there are positions to be filled at the Imperial Palace."

"Around the Emperor in Jerusalem?"

"Yes. There and at the much larger palace off world. Regents and such," she said. "And then there are other places," she added softly.

"Other places?" I asked. "Where besides at the Imperial court?"

"Other places. Other worlds."

"Like this one?"

"Yes."

"Oh. Perhaps I had better keep that in my private journal," I said.

"Yes, perhaps you should."

[N.D.] The Immortals seem to have experiences when they transport. When they are among us, we are happy. They do not all leave us at the same time. Some of them are always with us. Many believe that when they are gone, they are at the Imperial Court in Jerusalem. Elaine tells me that this is not always true. That not only can the Immortals travel anywhere in this world, but they can also go to another place where the Emperor is sometime in residence. This place, this next-door-place, is not far away but we can not enter it. I have asked Elaine many questions about this place, but she does not give very long answers to my questions. I long to go there. Sometimes I don't think I can stand it if I do not. I am trying . . .

"Excellency!"

"Yes, Gerald, I was trying to write."

"A thousand pardons, Excellency. I deemed this of significant importance."

Of course, Gerald is an excellent secretary. He would not interrupt my work needlessly.

"The angel, your angel Lucius, has brought someone that you will want to see."

I went to the outer chamber to find Lucius holding the arm of a young male mortal.

"The Metropolitan and Elaine send this man to you," Lucius said.

"Why?" I gestured.

"He is, unusual, as a mortal. You are to study him closely."

He did not look unusual to me and I sensed nothing extraordinary.

"What is you name?" I asked.

"William, Ma'am. I am sent to the Lord Metropolitan by her highness Janice to be with you."

"To be with me?"

"Yes, Ma'am."

What are the Immortals up to? Surely not a mate for me. Elaine and I have settled that. What is there about the boy that they want me to observe?

"How old are you?" I asked.

"Nineteen, Ma'am."

"What do you do?"

"I have dreams, Excellency."

"Dreams?"

"Yes, Excellency."

He paused.

"They seem to be unusual, Ma'am."

"Tell me about them."

"Well, at first I would know I was dreaming, but I couldn't remember them."

"Continue."

"Gradually, I became aware of what I was experiencing in my dreams."

" Let us sit and talk," I said.

"Yes, Ma'am. As I was saying, I became aware that I was traveling in my dreams."

"With an angel?" I was curious now as I have traveled with Lucius many times but I never remember anything about the journey.

"Sort of. I mean, I sense that there are angels nearby, although I do not always see them. But I do not believe that my body actually travels."

"Whether in the body or out of the body I can not tell," I muttered.

"Yes, Ma'am. It's, it's hard to be sure."

"That is a phrase of a Second Testament leader, "whether in the body or out of the body I can not tell." I told him.

"Yes, I understand."

He is a very amiable boy.

"At first I saw visions of the capitol."

"Jerusalem?"

"Yes, Ma'am. I even glimpsed the Emperor from a distance. But, then I began to see other places. At first I was not sure where these places were. Perhaps on the earth, sub-capitals or provinces of the Emperor. But I also glimpsed the Emperor in these places. I saw many Immortals but never a mortal. So I began to believe that these were the 'next-door-places' that we know are open to the Immortals."

"Go on," I said almost anxiously. Elaine knew that this was my passion.

"At first I had believed that I was seeing the Immortals inside some sort of rooms, but the walls were not distinct. I thought, at first, that they were merely individual palaces. The walls are covered with some sort of hangings, gossamer like. But just as there were no mortals present, there was also no outdoors as we know them. You know, fields with trees and grass and flowers."

"I see."

"I have been to this place many times in my dreams and I began to understand what it is. Excellency, it is a gigantic palace."

"A Palace?"

"Yes, a gigantic palace."

"How gigantic?"

"I can not tell. Perhaps larger than the whole earth."

Now that is large, I thought to myself.

"Yes, I believe that it is the real Emperor's palace. That the one in Jerusalem which is quite magnificent is only a tiny copy of this one in this 'next-door-place.' It is where the Immortals go to be with the Emperor without us. Only there, he is not exactly the Emperor. There they are, they are . . . family. They fellowship with him as brothers and sisters. There is no formality there like there is at court here. And I think, I think, . . .I'm not too clear on this Excellency. . . I think that the Emperor's Father is also nearby when they are together in this palace."

He stopped speaking and we both sat in silence for several moments. I was enthralled. I could not understand why this young man was allowed to see such things and I, the Spiritual Primate, was not. But I was thankful that Elaine had this young man sent to me. He looked at me with some anxiety and a question in his eyes and I realized that he was waiting to see if I actually believed him. I had been so absorbed in my own reaction that I had neglected to reassure him, not an acceptable attitude for someone in my position. I hurried to reassure him. I groped in my mind for his name.

" Wil,. . .William." His eyes brightened. "I am sure that this is a great gift that you have been given and I want to chronicle it as completely as possible and add these accounts of what you have seen, and possibly will yet see, to the sacred texts."

He looked relieved and surprised at the same time, relieved because I believed him and surprised that I wanted to put his dreams in the texts. I continued. "You must tell me more, everything. We will schedule sessions together. You will stay here at the residence."

Over the next weeks and months I chronicled every thing that William told me about his dreams. We met each morning while his memory of his dreams was still fresh. He did not have any waking visions. Everything came as he slept. In the day time, after our sessions, he seem quite normal. He loved to swim in my pool and play on my sporting courts. He read in my library and he even sang a few songs. He was always very respectful, even formal, to me even though we were close to the same age.

William explored extensively the magnificence of this "next-door-place" palace. It became obvious that a mortal lifetime would not be long enough to see it all. There were millions of rooms. These rooms were all gigantic and self lit, the walls actually glowed. The rooms could be used for any purpose and the Immortals had the ability to change them according to their wishes. Since William's visions or visits were limited in time he could never actually plumb the depths of the palace or even the rooms. Everywhere there was love among the Immortals. They all appeared to be pretty much the same age. Some of them had marks on their bodies which appeared to William as fine jewelry only a part of their flesh such as it is. We decided after a while that the markings were a reflection of wounds sustained for the Emperor in the past. Now they were beautiful jewelry. This jewelry does not appear on the Immortals we see here. Here they have only their symbols of office, coronets and scepters. Except for what Anna saw in the Emperor's hands and these marks were not jewelry, they were wounds, not even scars but the wounds themselves. Since Anna did not tell us any more, we can not say that they are exactly open wounds. Some of the rooms in this palace were assembly rooms and some were private rooms.

There were also hallways leading to rooms. There were angels in the hallways. These angels looked much like the ones we see here on earth, but they seemed to glow much brighter in this palace. The farther up in the palace you went the larger and brighter the rooms, not that the very lowest ones were in any way dull or small. The scale was simply greater that anything we can imagine. Sometimes there were bright colored lights in the walls. Sometimes these lights "danced." Some of the largest rooms were dining halls where the Immortals ate fine feasts with the Emperor. One time, while seeing a very high and magnificent and bright room, one wall seemed almost transparent and there was a great and mighty presence on the other side of this strange wall. William thought that it was the actual presence of the Emperor's Father. Near this wall the Emperor seemed to be teaching masses of Immortals. We wondered what the Immortals could be in need of learning. William could not hear what was being said. Lucius, in one of his rare talking periods, hinted that the Emperor was teaching the Immortals about His Father, their Father, and that this teaching would never end. A teaching that would never end? I wondered about this. How could we, or the Immortals, ever be complete if there was a teaching that would never end? But, I am convinced that Lucius is not capable of lying. William said that at one point he thought he remembered seeing the Emperor take a large group of Immortals through this wall into the presence of His Father.

My time with William was the high point of my days. Most of the time it was just me and William and Lucius. Lucius was quiet. William was duly respectful to Lucius as all mortals are to the angels in spite of the revelations that he has seen in his dreams. Mortals have all seen angels either at the Dais of some ruler or in their duties observing mortals or transporting them to trial. But since I am the only mortal with an angel of my own, most mortals are very cautious around them. Gradually William became more comfortable around Lucius.

09.12.657 C.R.   Today I have my meeting that I have each year with the Governor of the East coast of

North America, Over-Lord Janice Holland. I dress formally for the occasion at the Residence and Lucius takes me to the Dais of the Governor. My little niece and probable heir Mandie asked me about my robe. It is light blue with white borders and a bronze crest which is placed over the heart of the wearer. My ancestor May added the crest. The robe was given to my ancestor Mark on the occasion of his wedding. The crest is a simple bronze shield about five inches in height with a white open book in the center and the word "truth" under the book. It has been the official crest of my offices since May's time. I have added, with Elaine's permission, a thin red border around the crest to match the red belt that is tied around my waist when I wear the robe which highlights my office as the Spiritual Primate of the mortals on the earth.

Upon arrival at her Dais Lucius precedes me through the portal although I am not aware of this action. After I step out, I await a nod from the Governor in case she is in the midst of another matter. This day she was free at the moment of my arrival. The Dais was full of Immortals and the surrounding area was packed with mortals with the officials in the front of the crowd. I walk to the Dais and bow deeply to the Governor. She nods slightly. No amount of rank as a mortal ever puts us on an even keel with an Immortal. The Governor then thanks me for the past years' work. I thank her for the compliment and report briefly on the meetings that I have had during the year and offer my opinion as to the faithfulness of the reading of the ancient books and the writings of Anna and her successors by mortals. She then asks me to take a short stool next to her on the Dais and we all share some wine and cakes made especially for the occasion. This was my tenth appearance before the Over-Lord in this regard. The Metropolitan of Atlanta was there as usual smiling proudly. Elaine was with him. During the polite talk over refreshments the Over-Lord mentioned something that I had never heard before.

"Elaine, I know that you are particularly proud of Joan."

"Yes, Janice, she is very competent in her duties, very competent."

"As the Emperor's Legate in this matter and the one who appoints the successor you too are to be complimented."

"Me, Janice, why?"

Elaine did not seem at all surprised by this apparent slip of the tongue. I did notice that I was the only mortal close enough to hear it.

"Why? Because, sister, you have chosen and trained Anna herself and each of her successors for nine generations of mortals now. It is working out very well. I know that the Emperor is pleased. You might ask Him about it the next time you see him," Janice continued.

"Thank you, Janice. Indeed I will. We do live to please Him."

"Yes, indeed we all do. And is it not wonderful?"

All at the Dais agreed. I longed to meet the Emperor. Only Anna herself and May have had that privilege in our succession. William has not even seen him closely in his dreams. I have thought of telling Lucius to take me to the Imperial Court, but it is a legend among us that you only go there when invited and I have not been asked to go there. Anna met Him at the Dais of our Metropolitan but the Emperor has not visited the Metropolitan so far during my lifetime.

I have not mentioned Elaine's status to any mortals. My successor may reveal this from my private journals should she or he see fit. She is the Imperial Legate from the Emperor in charge of the Annatic line and also under Governor to the court of the Metropolitan Henry Sawyer. I do not believe that any of my predecessors have ever dreamed of the importance of our work, except maybe May. She is an ongoing wonder and a mystery, dear little May.

I have read May's account of her visit to Jerusalem over and over. Her description of the Throne area is a key. She said, "A wide permanent sort of portal is always open behind the throne. You can not see very far in because of a sort of mist or veil. But if you stand to the side of the audience chamber, you can tell that there is another throne back to back to the one here, or perhaps they have a common back, one throne with a seat on each side."

[N.D.] One morning William arrived at my study very excited.

"Excellency, I have had the most wonderful dream so far."

I motioned for him to sit and handed him a drink.

"It started again in one of the great hallways in the gigantic palace." He was so excited that he started talking before he found his seat and almost dropped his drink. I helped him and he continued to talk without stopping.

William continued, "I walked for what seemed to be miles. I passed a few people, Immortals, but as usual they did not acknowledge me; I don't think they see me. I took several turns; I don't know why I made the decisions that I did. Then at the end of the hall I saw two great doors. I walked up to them. The handles were low, at the normal height. I pressed down on the right one and pushed hard on the door. It glided open easily and gracefully and I went in. It was an enormous throne room. There were many beautiful large angels at various vertical levels in the room. The room was self-lighted and filled with a light mist. The smell was sweet and delightful. As I walked through the room unnoticed, I neared the throne itself. It was on a golden marble Dais. There were twelve steps up to the throne. The Emperor sat on the throne in his white robe. He was smiling a beautiful smile and everyone was delighting in His smile. As I approached from the side, I noticed a large open portal behind the throne. The throne on this side of the portal shared its back with another one on the other side. I could not see very far into the portal. There is a sort of a mist which functions as a veil, so I do not know where it led. There were no mortals on the side I was on in my dream, only the Emperor, Immortals and angels. The angels around the throne were different than any I have ever seen on earth. They hovered always and each had six wings. The wings are just a blur, but I could still count three pairs on the back of each angel."

I did not respond at first to William. I had to decide just what he was allowed to know. Obviously, the other side of William's throne is in the temple in Jerusalem. At that one place the seen and unseen worlds come together at the veil and the throne of the Emperor in both of His realms. What a beautiful creation. But how much of this can I tell to the world? This has always been a problem for the Keeper. We have always felt that some things were better left in the family journals, but, on the other hand, we have a duty to tell all that we can. I must ask Elaine. I sent William to rest while I considered it all.

I told Lucius to ask Elaine if I could see her. In about 30 minutes Elaine appeared.

"You did not have to come to me," I said. She sat next to me. I love her so.

"How often do you call? I am glad to come. What is it?" Elaine asked.

I showed her May's entry. I do not know if she had ever seen it before. When she finished, I told her about William's dream. She sat for a minute.

"I have been to that portal, the Throne Portal," Elaine said softly. "It is the only portal that we have to use. There is nothing in May's writing or William's dream that is not true. You do not know how much to publish."

I nodded.

"That has always been left to your line."

"I know. This time I am stumped."

"You meditate on it for a while," she touched my hand. "And I will ask the Emperor, if necessary." Before long she left.

I have often wished that we had the Helper, the Presence, that the Immortals had when they were mortal. We have the Emperor Himself, so I feel guilty when I think such thoughts. My line also has Elaine to help guide us and she is the Imperial Legate. I thought about this until bed time and slept soundly.

[N.D.] I fear that I have contributed to William's drive to learn more and more about what he was seeing in his dreams. I did now know that he had taken to strenuous exercise that would help him to sleep more often and for longer periods of time. It was during one of his reports that I realized how intense he had become. He was telling me about his wanderings in the halls of the palace behind the veil in his dreams. He had taken to reclining for his report and since he appeared to be more comfortable, I did not object.

"I know I have been down the same hallway many times. Don't ask me how I know because these halls all look so much alike, but I just know. I have been past the throne room as seen from the door off this hall several times and the large banquet room which has the strange bright wall which seems to lead to the presence of the Emperor's Father. No one, even the Immortals, can go in there except when they are with the Emperor. But last time I discovered something that I had not seen before. I say discovered but I realize that I have no control over where I go when I am on these sojourns, even though I sometime think that I choose which way to turn. For the first time I actually got to the end of this main hallway that I have been telling you about. don't know if I really went further or whether things changed. The entire palace there is so very immense, bigger than the whole world I am sure. I went through a door near the end and then the door at the end of this hall. The door near the end opened into the most enormous room I have ever seen. It was very bright and inhabited by myriads of angels. They were impossible to count. They hovered at many levels to near the top of the room but it was so high that I could not actually see to the top and they were in so deep that I could not see that wall either. They seemed content and quiet, but there was also a feeling that they wished they could have something to do. I believe it is the Emperor's Reserve of angels. It proves that there is no situation which would be too difficult for angels to deal with.

There is a simple door at the end of the hall. It looks like all the other doors in the palace, grand and solid. The door lever is ornate and golden like all the others. The door is not particularly wide and, like all the other doors, there is no lock. I put out my hand to open it and suddenly, in my dream, I became very hesitant. Somehow I knew that this door led to somewhere quite overwhelming. Slowly I worked up the courage. I touched the door lever. I push down gently almost hoping that it would not open. But the lever pushed easily and went completely down. I leaned against the door slightly. Like all the doors here it opened easily. I stepped out onto a balcony with a railing. There was nothing before me but worlds. Stars and worlds and lights by the millions. I moved to one side of the porch. It was attached to the side of the palace. I turned around to look at the palace itself and it was so far to the top or bottom or sides that I could not see the end of it. The porch was probably miles and miles high on the side of the palace. I was convinced of its enormity. I noticed a gate in the center of the railing around the porch. 'A gate to where,' I asked myself. There was nothing but space beyond. An Immortal came through the door. As usual no one sees me when I am there in my dreams. Maybe I am not really there, who knows? This Immortal moved directly to the gate and opened it and stepped out. Immediately he was gone and I knew that he was on one of those worlds that I could see in the distance. This must be how they leave the palace and travel to other worlds. Perhaps they rule there as well."

William seemed exhausted but he insisted that there was one more dream that was even more important. "I don't know why but I was beginning to think that I could have a limited amount of control on these trips," he continued. "The next time I found myself in this central hall I determined to wait outside the banquet room with the strange wall that led to the presence of the Emperor's Father. I found myself there in my next dream and I was able to stop and wait by the open door of this room. There was a banquet in progress. I could see the Emperor's table over near that wall and the thousands upon thousands of banqueters. Angels were bringing food in on great trays. A young Immortal woman came through the door and I begged her to take me to the Emperor's table. She was strangely able to hear and see me and she agreed. She took me right up to the Emperor's place and sat me beside Him. He did not turn or speak but in a few minutes he motioned for those right around Him to follow Him through the wall. I went along. I shouldn't have. I may never recover."

"William, William, you don't have to continue," I urged.

"Yes, just a little more."

I nodded.

"The Emperor's Father exceeds Him in Glory," William said. Then he started to cry. "You know the accounts of the Emperor here on earth, like when mother Anna saw him at the Dais."

"Yes."

"His Father radiates a light and a benign heaviness that is unbearable to mortals."

"Does He have a shape, a body?" I asked..

"Not exactly, but you can tell where He is concentrated. But it is all just too much!"

"What about the Immortals? When they are in the Presence?"

"They too seem overwhelmed, but it does them no harm. The Emperor is always teaching them something about His Father. But even they do not stay there for very long. Only the Emperor can bear constant exposure. But for us, for us, Keeper, it is just too much."

William broke into uncontrollable sobs and I could not get him to stop. These escalated into a seizure and then he passed out. I was very frightened and sent Lucius to ask Elaine to come. I had never thought that there could be too much goodness in our lives.

Elaine arrived before William woke up, I think it was only about 6 or 7 minutes. I explained what had led up to this.

"I am afraid that he has gotten over zealous," Elaine said. She laid her hand over his heart.

I agreed. "What should we do?" I asked.

He began to come around. We both comforted him. He began to recognize us both.

"Keeper. Excellency, I . . . what?"

"Just relax," I said.

After a few minutes he was ready for some water.

"You must stop pushing yourself," I told him. Surprisingly he offered no argument.

"I have strengthened your body," Elaine said. "But you must do as the Keeper says. Do not expect any more dreams until I permit it."

William agreed. Evidently this last dream had totally drained him. Elaine signaled me to walk her to the door. "He will not dream for some time now. But he will rest easily. He will not be allowed near the Emperor's Father again. He can not endure the fullness of it. Even we must be careful. Keep me informed on how he is doing?"

"Of course." Then she was gone.

10.17.660 C.R.   William stayed at the residence and continued in some of the activities that he had enjoyed at first, such as playing on my courts and swimming in my pool. He even got back to the library and did some research on his own. We visited and shared together every few days, sometimes once a week, sometimes twice. He seemed contented enough and I saw no reasons to be concerned for him. Then he began to spend more time out. This did not concern me as he was a grown man and I had offered him my hospitality freely. Before long he did not come back to the residence every night. Then he would only be there one or two nights a week. I thought of telling Lucius to go invisible and follow him, but this seemed out of character for him and I had never done this before with anybody. I was, however, growing quite concerned so I decided to ask Lucius what he knew without first instructing him to follow William outside the residence.

"He is not doing well, Keeper," was Lucius' response.

"Go on."

"He is meeting with a group that induces dreams and visions with the use of certain herbs and chemicals."

I was shocked. Why should such a naturally gifted person resort to such things? "How much exactly have you seen," I asked.

"I have accompanied him several times while you were sleeping, Keeper. He could not see me and I have observed all these things myself."

"Observed them yourself as compared to . . . .?" I asked.

"As compared to accessing a report from the Legions' vault."

"The   Legion's   vault?"

"Yes, Keeper."

Angels can have a frustrating habit of never saying more than was necessary to us mortals. Generally, Lucius had been trained by my predecessors to do better than this, but he could still be frustrating.

"Why Lucius, why . . . the Legions' vault? I, I am . . ." I was almost at a loss for words I was so frustrated and bordering on being angry which I am well aware has absolutely no effect on angels. I started again, "I am the Keeper, the ninth in succession since Mother Anna, and I have never been informed of the Legions' vault of records. Why?" I knew the answer before he responded and began to shake my head in agreement before he was finished.

"You did not ask, Keeper."

It seems that all I have ever learned, or that any human would learn for that matter, would always be a game of 20 questions, or 100 questions or thousands. But I persevered none the less.

"What is the vault, er . . . like?"

"The term 'vault' is just a term, Keeper. There is no actual vault in the human sense."

"That I am fully prepared to believe. Go on, tell me more. Do not stop until I bid you to."

"Yes, Keeper, I will tell you all that I can on this matter. There are certain angels in each Legion who have the duty to store any information that might prove useful to us. This is based primarily on experience. We go to them when we need information. Much of this information is gleaned from our routine patrols over the centuries. There are connecting vaults between each legion of angels to facilitate sharing of information. I simply inquired about William's activities. Then I followed him myself. I would think it wise for you to intervene, Keeper, before he does himself harm."

I considered this a valuable and succinct report and I could not be bothered with anymore discussion about these angelic vaults. I had to find William and intervene, with Elaine if necessary.

"He is sleeping in his room here at the residence, Keeper. He was out very late last night." Now he was anticipating my questions. It seemed that it was either one extreme or another. I went to William's door and knocked firmly.

"Uh, . . . who?" was the response.

"It is Joan. I must talk to you."

"Just, . . .just a moment, Excellency. I must make myself decent."

There was considerable bumping around in his room and a wait of several minutes. I leaned against the wall to wait.

"I am so sorry, please come in," a hastily prepared William said as he opened the door. He offered me the only chair that did not have clothing or something on it."

"William, you might as well know that I am aware that you have been inducing dreams and visions with herbs and chemicals," I proclaimed. I tried very hard to keep my voice calm.

There was a short pause. He looked directly at me. His brown eyes were very bloodshot and blurry. "Excellency, I, . . . I am sorry to have disappointed you. It was just that after all those wonderful dreams I became desperate when they stopped. I had to try something and I found out from some acquaintances that there were places where mortals did this. I sought them out." He paused. "How did, how did you. . .?" He looked at Lucius who had come with me. I had not noticed. "Of course, the angel," he said accusingly.

"Now, William, Lucius does what he thinks is best for me and my house."

"Yes, Excellency." He was retreating into formalism, so I changed my tone.

"It is just that I value you and care for you, William," I said in a positively motherly tone.

"Yes, Joan, I know that you do. It is hard when a person has been blessed with such dreams to do without them. It's like a addiction."

"Tell me truthfully, William, do the herbs and chemicals help?"

"They are mostly herbs, and they do help some. But mostly they are a disappointment."

"Because the dreams aren't so good?"

"Yes, with them I do not seem to actually leave my own mind. It is just a rehash of what I have already seen."

"What did they ever do? There are reports of these in the ancient records right here in my own library. It seems like they were always a disappointment."

"Yes, yes, that is actually where I got into this. From the ancient records here. But in ancient times there were others, a sort of angels, probably not good ones, who, er, . . . helped."

"Helped?"

"Yes, once the mind is loosened from the soul by the herbs, these sort of angels would meet it and help it to see beyond itself. Now it is only what is inside repeated over and over and changed around."

"I see. Why do you suppose this is?"

He thought a while. "I suppose this is so because these connecting spirits are no longer available. They are bound away with the others."

"Then this is not a good thing, is it?"

"No, but I need released from this longing, Joan."

"Lucius, get Elaine. We will be in my parlor."

I had William cleaned up and in decent clothes when Elaine arrived. She knew it was urgent when I sent for her instead of letting her set the meeting place. Lucius had briefed her.

"Now, William," she said after we had gone over it all again, "I will release you from this longing." She put her hand on his chest, He exhaled deeply and seemed to be at peace. In a few seconds his eyes appeared clearer. "You will have to occupy yourself with other things for quite a while now. I do not know if you will ever dream again. I had you brought to Elaine from your village when you first started dreaming because it was a gift and she wanted to know much of what you were seeing and hearing in your dreams. But you obviously can not contain it, at least not at this time. I am going to send you to a sort of school that the Over-Lord Janice has. There are other seekers like yourself there and they all receive a lot of positive direction. Now, I make no promises, but if you are to dream again, you must first learn maturity and discipline. It is your choice, this school or your own village."

"I choose the school, Excellency," William answered.

Elaine turned to me. "I will give you this day and tomorrow to say your good-byes, dear. Morning after next Lucius will take him. He will be fine there and you may visit him at your discretion."

I nodded and hugged her.

"I have missed you much lately, Joan. I want to have tea with you more often."

"That would be very nice. Please, don't let it be long."

"I won't, dear." Then she was gone.

William and I had a very pleasant evening and next day. He was very relaxed and, I think, relieved. Late in the second day when we were saying our good-byes Lucius approached us. I knew what he wanted so I stepped back.

Lucius opened a portal and they departed on schedule. I instructed Lucius to remind me to have him take me to visit William in two weeks and every month thereafter.

02/01/671 C.R. My fiftieth birthday.
I have finally found an old notebook telling me about Elaine's mortal life. She has never volunteered this information to any of my line. However, all of the materials found in my now extensive library have been given in good faith and I have full authority to read all of it and enter the information in records public or private. This little notebook is extremely soiled. It looks to be in her own hand. She probably did not have access to a better book to use for a dairy. It is held together by a coiled wire and is about six inches high and four inches wide. Elaine was the second daughter of a farmer in the mid-nineteenth century in Georgia. She had always loved the Emperor and volunteered at an early age to be a missionary to Africa. She went out with the full expectation that she would die in Africa. While there, she made many converts and caught a plague disease which was prominent in that era. She ran a very high fever for some time and final prayers were said over her. She was expected to die. Some of her converts prayed for her. The other missionaries thanked them politely and started digging her grave. The next morning she was much better. She was breathing easily and her fever was gone. She recovered and went back to her work making converts to the Emperor and taking care of and teaching the children in the area. She was captured by a rival tribe and treated terribly. They violated her and beat her. She was almost dead again when the missionaries found enough soldiers to rescue her. Again her converts prayed for her and she was restored. They took her to a doctor in a large city and he said that Elaine was healthy and still a virgin. This was a miracle. Elaine said that the Emperor had restored her entirely, emotionally and

physically. The government of the country that she was in was overthrown by rebel powers and she was forced to return to Georgia. At this time her home country was very near to civil war. Because of Elaine's love for Africans she was distressed by the slavery which she saw around her. She became very active in the system that transported slaves out of the area and placed them farther North. She helped many of them to escape until she was discovered by those who were against her work and they beat her to death on a deserted road in Buckhead. It is the Emperor's way to appoint Immortals to govern where they have been Martyred. The postscript to Elaine's dairy was probably written by a friend who worked with her in smuggling slaves North. This person says that Elaine would have preferred to die in Africa, but this was not the Lord's will. This is the way pre-Reign people referred to the Emperor who was invisible then. It is possible that Elaine would then have preferred to govern somewhere in Africa now, but she has been appointed Governor of Buckhead under the Metropolitan Henry Sawyer under the Over-Lord Janice Holland of the East Coast under the Hemispheric Viceroy Luis Cepata under the Emperor who reigns from Jerusalem. This is our beloved Elaine. She died at the age of 31. She was raised at the Glorious Return of the Emperor. We love her dearly.

[personal note: I will not release this in my public journal, however, I believe that Elaine's position as Imperial Legate with the oversight of my offices is an additional honor due to her work in Africa.]

08/11/675 C.R.   In my efforts to develop as much material as I can in my own lifetime I have been reviewing the private journals of my father and his predecessors as far back as Anna herself. Anna once questioned why the Empire existed. At first this may sound like a stupid question. But when we know that the Immortals would all rather be with the Emperor in the "away" or the "next-door-place," the question can start to look rational. Anna was sure that it was not because the Emperor wants to lord it over us. Even His Princes do not seem to need the job. It is good for us, however, as Anna has pointed out. We benefit from the peace and power of the Emperor's kingdom. Life is good for mortals. You realize this when you study the history of pre-Reign earth as I have. Even though this may be true, it does not seem like enough of a reason. I believe that in my studies I have cobbled together a reason that would be important to the Emperor and to His Father and to all the Immortals. It was owed to the Emperor as a man. He came as a man and was treated despicably by the mortals of his time even though He has always been good and shares the very life of His Father intimately. These mortals that treated him so still lie in their graves. Our Immortals were loyal to him while he was here as a man and all the time that He was gone back to His Father. They were transformed, both the dead and the living, at his Glorious Return almost 700 years ago now. I believe that in the heart and mind of the Emperor's Father the Reign is owed to the Emperor as a man. As God he can take what he wants and needs no satisfaction. As a man it is owed to Him. This is my conviction formed after many years in my office and much intense research. I hope that my successors will receive it and pass it on.

[N.D.]   I am feeling very old and lonely today. I have just finished my quarterly address to the people which I began doing three years ago. I speak to them from the amphitheater near the Over-Lord's Dais in New York and it is published and disseminated around the world by the mortals in my publications department. We have never been allowed the electronic means that existed before the Reign. It seemed to do more harm than good. Also, that kind of communication is taken care of by the angels and the Immortals when it is necessary. The residence has been greatly enlarged to accommodate all of my staff and I seem to have many more servants than I can use. I find it necessary as every influential mortal house wants the honor of having someone in my residence in any position that is available. So I have created positions that I do not need. When Lucius returned me to the residence after my speech, the main hall was full of staff and servants. As usual they welcomed me back with cheers and applause.

"Friends and fellow servants," my major domo announced, "once again our mistress, the Keeper of the Ancient Books, the Primary Interpreter of the books of Anna, the Chronicler of Imperial truth, and the Spiritual Primate of the mortals on the earth has brought great enlightenment to our people. May she live long and continue to instruct us well."

I made it through the formalities and said that I needed to retire to my room and rest. Where did I find that windbag? How had it all grown so large? If I had done something wrong, surely Elaine would have corrected me.

[N.D.] "They find it necessary," Elaine said. I had asked to see her. Lucius took me to her house near the Dais. "Joan, we do not want to suppress the mortals. They need to be free to establish certain institutions so long as they respect the Emperor and us properly. You can cut back on your house if you wish. It is all under your authority."

Elaine makes me feel young. She never ages, she never changes. Right now she appears nearly 40 years my junior. I find this refreshing.

"Yes, Elaine. Thank you. I may make some changes. Or I may leave them to my successor. Will that be Mandie?"

"Yes. You have trained your niece well and she is of good character. You could share some duties with her to intensify her training."

She looked at me very kindly. My days are nearing an end. I am relieved.

[N.D.] During my regular weekly conference with Elaine a few days later I asked if we could talk on personal matters after the work was finished. We were at her house near the Dais and she instructed her staff that we were not to be disturbed.

I took Elaine's hand; she always allowed this but I seldom reached out to her in that manner. "You and I both know, Elaine, that my days are nearing an end and I would like to know what it is like to die," I asked.

"Dear Joan, no sooner do I get well acquainted with a Keeper than you have to leave. I wish I could give you an account of dying in peace, but I can not. As you know, I died in the midst of pain and violence, and death was a welcome release. Since it was for my testimony to the Emperor, I have no regrets. But you will go in the midst of the peace of the Reign. Would you talk to a friend of mine who died in peace about this?"

"Yes, if this person is your friend, I would like that."

"She is; she is my dear friend and we knew each other as mortals for a short time. We are closer now than we were then. I don't mean in the way that we are all closer now, but that we spend time together now and have grown to be great friends."

"You do that? I mean Immortals?"

"Yes, we do. In most ways we are still human."

"I don't know why I never realized that," I responded.

Elaine's friend was sent for as we talked and soon two Immortals arrived.

"Joan, this is my friend Mona and another friend Jacob," Elaine said. I had not expected two of them. They were both Immortals but not rulers or princes. We all nodded to each other.

"Joan, please forgive me for surprising you," Jacob said quickly. "You see I came also because I was transformed at the Glorious Return. Mona here was raised at that time and we thought that both of our stories might be of interest to you as the Keeper."

"Oh, but Joan's question was not as the Keeper, Jacob," Elaine added.

"I am so sorry," Jacob said and began to rise.

"No, please stay," I said. "I would very much like to hear about both of your experiences." Jacob sat back down and Mona began.

"I lived in Elaine's time. We met at a few believer's meetings and were on several prayer teams together. That, well, that was the way we talked to the Emperor in those times."

"I am familiar with that," I said.

"Of course, you are," Mona said. "You are the Keeper, aren't you?"

"Well, things were not easy then, but I was never given a particularly difficult time. Elaine was taken at a much younger age than I was. I lived to be an old woman. My mortal children always took very good care of me," Mona continued. "I simply died in my sleep as you are most likely to do. I went to bed one night feeling fine. I said my prayers and went to sleep soon thinking about Je, er, the Emperor. Then I thought I was waking up when I became aware of a bright light. And, there was my mother. She had been gone for some years. She hugged me and welcomed me and said that she would take me to see Him. All my aches and pains were gone. I had had arthritis, a pain in the joints, for years. I realized that I could see very clearly out of both eyes; this was also new. I was aware of myself like when you used to roll your eyes as a child to be aware that you are looking out of a body; but there was actually no body there. I recognized my mother when I looked at her but she said that she was just as unaware of a body as I was. But we were there. We were conscious. The Emperor had a body that was solid, but he was the only one then. All I remember was being happy and contented and time did not seem to pass or matter. Then when the trumpet blew I found myself back inside a body very much like the one I had had before except that this one was very light and durable. I was then Immortal as I am now. Does that help at all?"

"Yes, it does, but how do I know if it will be that way for me? I mean the trumpet has already blown. What is to become of us, we mortals now?"

Elaine took over the conversation, "Joan, I will tell you all that I can. In the first place, no mortals who have died have been added to our numbers as corporal Immortals since the trumpet sounded. But there is a place on, on the "away" side, where we are not permitted to go or to see into. The Emperor does go there. I believe . . . I believe, and I want to be so very careful here, that those mortals who are faithful to him here are in that place after they die just as Mona was in such a place after she died. I have no other insights for you except that I have heard his Excellency Gabriel speaking to the Emperor when we are "away" about another sounding of the trumpet. You do not live in the age of faith as we did. The Emperor is physically present here as we are. But He is the same man; he is the same God. And He will do what is right. Does this give you any comfort, my dear Joan?"

"Yes, Elaine it does."

"I am so very glad." We embraced again. I embraced Mona as well.

There was a period of silence before Jacob spoke. "I, Joan, was transformed at the sound of the trumpet."

"Yes, tell me please," I said.

"Well, I was going about my daily routine. Things had been very difficult and some of us were hiding in some caves near our city. There was no other place to live but we had managed by His grace to scratch out a living in the hills. We hoped and prayed every day for the return of the Emperor. Then early one morning the trumpet was heard all over the world. Gabriel shouted the greatest shout ever uttered and we began to rise. As we rose, there was a tingling feeling all over my body that lasted only for a part of a second, "a twinkling of an eye," and I realized that my body had changed. We were so glad to see the Emperor that we just rejoiced in his presence for a while. Time became unimportant."

"Anna experienced that temporarily," I jumped in.

"Yes, yes she did," Jacob said. "I read that."

I was surprised again. The Immortals read the Annatic journals.

Jacob continued, "Then soon we were all being given our tasks for the Reign. Many of us have tasks even though we do not all rule."

I nodded and thanked them all. Soon Jacob and Mona opened a portal and departed. I sat in silence with my friend Elaine for quite a while.

-[N.D.] My sister Marie's daughter Mandie is a good girl. She has attained womanhood now and she is very interested in the work. She is a tall girl with fair skin and hair; very graceful. I am short and dark and have always struggled with my weight. She will probably deal with the ceremonial portions of the office much more gracefully than I. She is also a capable researcher and scholar. She says that she will remain unmarried just as I have, but that will remain to be seen. If too many of us remain unmarried, the succession will get complicated although I am sure that the ageless Elaine who watches over our work will be able to deal with it all quite well.

[N.D.] Several days later I was awakened by someone opening the curtains in my room which allowed a brilliant flow of sunlight. In my awakening stupor the first thought that crossed my mind was that I had died in my sleep but it soon became obvious that this was not so. My arm ached where I had been sleeping on it. My next emotion was of anger. Who dare's awaken me before I am done sleeping? Then I looked at the figure with the bright sunlight behind it standing in my window. It looked like the shape of Elaine. It was Elaine.

"I must ask you to arise, Joannie," she said.

Have we gone back in time, I thought. Joannie?

"Come on, up, up, you have a lot to do."

I squinted up at her to make sure that this was Elaine as any of my servants would be in for a severe tongue lashing. But, sure enough, it was Elaine. I struggled to arise but my arm gave way. I thought that maybe now she would realize how old I was and take pity on me. After all I was not a forever young and strong Immortal.

"Joan, are you in pain?" she asked as she hurried to my bed.

"Yes, somewhat, I have had some aching in my joints of late."

I was still perplexed as to why she was here and what she wanted at this early hour.

"It is almost the third hour of the day," she said as she took my arm with both hands. "This aching must stop," she said. She rubbed my arm and touched me with her hands gently and tastefully from head to toe. I felt very warm for a few seconds. Then she arose and pulled me up by both hands.

"Now stretch," she commanded.

I obeyed. I felt strong. I felt twenty years younger.

"Good," Elaine said. She put her hands on my shoulders.

"Dear Joan. I am sorry, but I can not allow you to be old just yet," she said. She was smiling. "You are not yet replacable."

"But Mandie, Mistress?" I asked. Having been treated like a child I began talking like one.

"It's still Elaine, dear. Mandie can accompany you constantly from now, but you are still the Keeper. She can learn on the job, but she must remain silent most of the time. There are some things to be done and I can not wait for her to get the necessary experience in order to begin. Now take your morning bath and dress and meet me in your breakfast room."

"I thought you were resigned to my death. Mona and Jacob, and . . ."

"I was, but I have been corrected. The Emperor wants you to serve a while longer."

"Yes, fine," I responded.

She walked out.

I could have been dreaming except that the curtains were still fully opened and I felt so wonderful. Again I obeyed. During my bath I remarked to myself that I had simply gotten too important in my own eyes. I was still a mortal under Elaine's supervision. I would be ready for any thing that she or the Emperor wanted me to do.

When I got to the breakfast room, Elaine was drinking some grape juice; she loved grape juice. My breakfast was ready but it was not my usual dry toast and tea. My cook, Yvonne, had a slightly perplexed look on her face.

"I had her prepare you something with more energy in it." Elaine said.

I thought it looked to be enough for two or three people.

"Help me," I said motioning towards my plate. There was meat and grains and fruit. More than I could possibly eat.

Elaine ate some of it, but as soon as I started I found that I was very hungry and soon devoured it all. Mandie showed up in the middle of it. She looked at my plate in surprise.

"Aunt Joan. Good morning. Mistress Elaine. So good to see you." She was a singularly beautiful and intelligent girl. We both embraced her as I continued eating. She glanced at my plate more than once. She asked Yvonne for some fruit and pealed it perfectly and ate.

"Elaine has given me a major healing." I said as I pulled my napkin out of its ring and wiped my face. "Something's up." She made one of those "what in the world" faces that she is so good at. What a girl!

"Aunt Joan, that's wonderful. You must feel fantastic."

"Yes, indeed. I do. All the aches and pains are gone. I feel twenty years younger. I think I am twenty years younger. I guess I don't get to leave yet. Sorry to delay your appointment. But she tells me that we are to be together constantly now."

"Great! Aunt Joan, I am in no hurry to succeed you. Believe me, it scares the daylights out of me. Mistress Elaine, " she glanced in her direction, "this angel has told me that we have a lot to do." I recognized one of Elaine's messenger angels who had arrived with Mandie.

I sat and watched Elaine. It was her turn to tell us what was happening.

"There is another budding rebellion," Elaine began. "It is on the Eastern coast of the far Eastern continent. It is very well shielded and quite large and it is still growing . . .Yes, Joan . . ."

I had motioned to interrupt. "Elaine, when you say it is well shielded, does that mean that you, the Immortals have not known about it from the beginning?" I was somewhat perplexed and it undoubtedly showed on my face.

"By shielded I mean that loyal mortals do not seem to be aware of it until they are about ready to join it. I must confess, I have been here now almost 700 years and I can never understand why the mortals would want to rebel. They have everything. There is perfect peace and abundance and justice in the kingdom. But still almost every generation another rebellion is discovered. The great evil Cherub and his followers are bound away, far away, we can not even go or see where they are. Yet in the heart of some mortals there is the urge to rebel. But I do want to be clear in answering your question, Joan. The Emperor always knows everything."

"The angels tell Him," I interrupted.

"Sometimes, but mostly His . . . His Brother tells Him. His Brother is all over the world and knows everything while the Emperor remains in Jerusalem or beyond the veil with us."

"Elaine, I am the Keeper and I am old for a mortal and I do not know about the Emperor's Brother, who . . . "

She raised her hand and I closed my mouth.

"Joan, you know about the Helper, before the return? Sometimes called the 'Presence'?"

"Yes. He is like the Emperor. He lived within you and the other Immortals when you were mortal."

"He still does. But he is also everywhere. He has no form."

"Like the Emperor's Father."

"Yes, but the Father is always beyond the veil and the Emperor is usually in Jerusalem or beyond the veil with us. The Emperor's Brother is everywhere and knows everything that is going on. As a result then, the Emperor and the Father also know as they are never separated. Often they inform the angels instead of the other way around."

I felt like the youngest of mortals. I glanced at Mandie. She was smiling but seemed to be taking it all in quite gracefully.

"Now, Joan, Mandie, to continue," Elaine sat up very straight and it was obvious that she would not be interrupted again. "We can, of course, just go in there and stop all of it. We can judge and then execute the leaders. We can even send the Prince Michael or an archangel in with some legions and quash the entire thing. They are not aware that we know anything about it. But the Emperor does not want to handle it that way. He wants to separate those who have been deceived from the true rebellious leadership. He wants you to go, take Mandie, and find your way into this group and try to disarm it and lead the deceived out before the true leaders are dealt with."

I kept a straight face. She had never asked me to do anything like this before.

"I know I have never asked you to do anything like this before, Joan, but each rebellion since the return has been dealt with differently. The results have also varied. This is important to the Emperor. Somehow, he is judging the hearts of mortals during His reign. So we do not ask why he wants it handled this way."

"Until you are beyond the veil with Him, and then you no longer care," I inserted with a smile. Elaine smiled back, this had become sort of a private joke between us. I did not fully understand it with my mind, but I did in my heart because I knew Elaine. Mandie just kept smiling.

"Yes, yes, and this time seems a bit unusual to us as well. But He always knows best. Now, He wants you . . ."

"The Emperor asked for me? . . . Sorry, I interrupted again," I said.

"He did, Joan. You and Mandie. My instructions for you are directly from Him."

I was smiling as broadly as Mandie by now except that at that last remark by Elaine, Mandie was now showing some tears as well around those gorgeous luminous blue eyes of hers.

"The Over-Lord in the area is Li Chen and the Metropolitan is Su Ming of Nanking."

I chuckled at "Su Ming of Nanking". "Sorry," I said.

Elaine continued patiently, "You will find a reason to visit them. Lucius will go with you as usual, but he will make himself invisible when you think it is best if he suspects something. You can command him to appear at anytime and he will appear brightly if it is appropriate. Of course, this will put a completely different complexion on things if you are trying to infiltrate their organization, so be careful when you tell him to appear. You may indicate some sympathy with their causes in order to gain entrance to their meetings, anything short of outright rebellion. You should be able to get in and using your credentials convince many of them to do the right thing. The Over-Lord and the Metropolitan will both be aware of what is going on and you may actually be contacted by the Emperor's Brother while you are there. Mandie should be included in everything that you do because this is a rare training event and should not be passed over for her. There is a minimum of danger as Lucius will always be nearby and the Presence is always near."

"Are you all right with this so far?" Elaine asked.

"Yes, yes, I'm fine. Mandie?" I glanced at my niece.

"Yes, Aunt Joan, I'm fine. It is so exciting. I am fine, Mistress Elaine," she answered beaming.

"You might as well call me Elaine. We will be seeing a lot of each other from now on."

"I will try, . . . Elaine." They smiled at each other and I was very happy for Mandie. Now she would have Elaine as her friend always.

"Now," Elaine began again. "Just so you will know what it is like to be aware that the Emperor's Brother is near, I have been permitted to take you into the Presence."

Mandie and I rose to go expecting Elaine to open a portal and take us somewhere. But she did not rise. We sat down again. Elaine closed her eyes and laid her hands on her lap palms up.

"Almighty One," she began. "Please show these dear mortals what it is like to be in the Presence, your Presence."

No sooner had Elaine said these words than I felt like all the breath had left my body. I heard Mandie gasp and looked her way. She was smiling and glowing and I suppose that I was as well. There was a sweet honey-like presence in and around us and it was very still. I began to laugh way down deep in side. When it became audible, I opened my eyes, I had not noticed that I had closed them, and looked toward Elaine for fear that I was being somehow disrespectful. Elaine nodded back and smiled and I knew that it was all right. I looked at Mandie, her eyes were still closed.   Then Elaine spoke softly. "This little sisters, is the joy of the Presence." I had never heard her call any mortal a sister. "There are other forms of the Presence which are meant to guide you."

"This means 'proceed'."

The Presence changed to an urging feeling and then increased to a stronger urging, a compelling. I almost felt pushed off my chair, but I was not afraid.

"This means 'stop'."

The Presence was strong, like a hand in front of my face. Unmistakable. Yet it was peaceful.

"This means 'not now'."

It was a strange combination of "stop" and "proceed." The "stop" sensation was first. Then I was overcome with the "proceed" sensation. Then they both lingered.

"Either of these can apply to whatever you are doing at the time. If you are speaking, it will apply to speaking. If you are walking, it will apply to walking. And so forth."

"This means 'not to fear'."

The peace of the Presence was so magnified and distinct that no explanation of what it meant was really necessary.

"This means 'danger'."

I shivered. I felt assurance but I also felt slightly afraid and almost guilty. It was if the greatest danger was not from rebels but from disrespecting the Emperor or His Father or His Brother.

"We don't think that many of the rebels speak the universal language, so the Presence will interpret for you and put the words that you need in your mouths." Elaine said. "Don't worry, it will be easy. It will seem natural. It is a joy working with the Presence. As you know, in our mortality we called Him, the Helper, and very, very few mortals are allowed to experience Him these days. "There are other guidance impulses, but they will be easy to understand when the time comes. With Lucius invisible you will need instruction from "the Presence." Elaine paused. "But remember, He is Divine. He is not your servant like Lucius."

We looked back at her and nodded. It was a lot to take in at once.

"Elaine, is this how you were guided as a mortal?" I asked.

"Yes, the Presence was always with us and we learned that we had to follow Him very closely if we wanted to survive. You and Mandie will be in no real danger, but He will guide you throughout this mission."

"I read in May's private journal that she experienced the Presence," I said.

"Yes, she did," Elaine answered.

"However, she was very special, spiritual," I added.

"She was, but she is not the only spiritual mortal that ever lived during the Reign," Elaine answered with a smile.

"When shall we leave?" I asked.

"First of all, Mandie needs to move into the residence with you on a permanent basis. I have already spoken with her mother and it is all arranged."

There was a sudden clamor at the front entrance as the porters arrived with Mandie's things. She had a lot of personal things for a twenty year old woman. The servants showed them through and the porters glanced into my sitting room as they passed. When they saw Lucius and Elaine, they moved right along. I was again amazed at the speed at which things moved when Elaine was of a mind to do something.

"You will need to be briefed on many details before you go," Elaine said and she glanced at Lucius.

We moved into my private office as I thought I would have to write many things down. Before long Lucius returned with two well groomed Oriental mortals. They bowed respectfully.

"Keeper, we are at your service," they said.

They nodded to Mandie, "Keeper Heiress," they said.

That was a new term. It was fine with me. I sent for drinks and Elaine waved good bye for now. She was gone. I motioned for them to sit down. They waited for me to pick up my pen and pad.

09/01/688   C.R.   Metropolitan Su Ming of Nanking is adorable. I did not remember ever meeting her before. She is so tiny and gentle and pretty. However, her firmness is legend as a ruler. The Over-Lord is a large man and almost frightening to look at, but he has a truly gentle heart. At first I had to remind myself that any Over-Lord would have suffered a lot for the Emperor as a mortal. We arrived at the Metropolitan's Dais and the Over-Lord was waiting for us there. As this was the official part of the visit Lucius was visible.

"Metropolitan Su, we are honored to be at your court," I said. "Metropolitan Sawyer sends his love."

I turned to the Over-Lord, "Prince Li, I am honored," I said and I bowed slightly.

"You are most welcome, Keeper," the Metropolitan said. She motioned me to sit on a seat beside her. The Over-Lord was on her other side. Mandie sat on the floor beside my feet. This was another new honor for me. It was usually me on a stool beside Elaine.

In private the Metropolitan told us that one of the mortals at her own court was known by the Immortals to be heavily involved with the rebels. His name was Lin Pao. Pao was a young man and he worked at the court as a supply supervisor. It was his job to procure food and clothing articles for the mortal members of the court. The Immortals in most courts like to live close to the people and so they share some of the things that were supplied for the mortals. Pao had to travel in connection with this job, so he was away for a day or two at a time quite often. No one was concerned that he procured food since the Immortals could not be poisoned and they would heal any mortals at court that started showing symptoms of poisoning. Generally rebel groups disliked Court mortals as they considered them to be traitors against their own kind. Mandie made it her mission to get to know Pao. It did not take her long to succeed. Although she was considerably taller than Pao, that did not seem to bother him. He thought of himself as a big man if not a tall one. Mandie walked the line between sympathy and rebellion and was soon invited to a meeting. At this meeting she met several dozen young rebels and was invited to attend again.

"I don't understand it, Aunt Joan," she told me back at our rooms at the Metropolitan's residence. "Their complaints seem so silly, things like 'we have the right to run our own country' and 'it isn't fair that we should be mortals and they are Immortal.' I mean, what can they do to change their mortality? What can any of us do? Anyway, why shouldn't the Immortals be in control. We have a hard time even providing generational continuity. You have been a good Keeper. When you die, it will take me decades to get back to where you are right now in capability and wisdom and, and . . . everything."

"These are things that lie in the human heart, Mandie. They don't ever seem to change." I leaned back in my chair.

"Why do you suppose, Aunt Joan, that the Emperor is dealing with this growing rebellion in this way? We know that He could shut it down in a matter of seconds."

"I'm not sure, Mandie. I believe it has something to do with revealing the thoughts of the human heart like Elaine said. In the years that I have lived I have learned that each generation has to fight the same battles over and over again. You remember Mark's testimony. He tried to run from his calling and he was Anna's own son. The Emperor may think that most of these young people aren't really that bad. But if His angels or Immortals simply shut it down, nothing is salvaged out of it. You know that before the Return He was called the Redeemer. It does put a great deal of pressure on my office to bring about the desired results though."

"I believe we can do it, Aunt Joan. The Presence is with us."

"That's my girl." We put our hands in our laps palms up hoping to enjoy the Presence, and sure enough, we felt Him strongly with us; peace prevailed, and what a peace.

"I am serious, Aunt Joan. I can feel the encouragement of the Presence right now, can't you?"

"Yes, yes I can. Since you just spoke, it's now kind of a 'can do' light-hearted feeling that is serious at the same time."

"Yes, that's it. We'll do it, with His help."

"It's amazing how He enables us to hear and speak their language."

"It is. I have been practicing with one of the under Governors. She knows our mission and is glad to help me," I said.

"Is it her native language?"

"Yes. She speaks the universal language, but she spent her mortality speaking this language. You have had more opportunity to use the gift though with these young people. You never falter?"

"Not really. They are a little surprised that I can speak it. I guess they just presume that as the Keeper Heiress that I speak a lot of languages."

Mandie went to enough meetings with Pao that they began to trust her. She started to mention that I was someone who could "understand" their feelings. She kept mentioning this until she got a chance to address the entire meeting one night. She recited it all to me. I knew that she had a good memory, but I did not know it was this good.

- "The Keeper come here?" one young man exclaimed. "She'll come with that angel of hers, what's his name, Lucius, and we'll all end up executed. No, no, that is out of the question."

"But what if she is really sympathetic?" a young woman asked. Some of us still think that we could get some considerations if we went to the Metropolitan or the Over-Lord about these things."

"No, no, the same young man answered again. We're in this to the end. If we're caught, we know what it will mean. It's all or nothing."

"What does that mean?" another young man asked. "All or nothing. We are no match for them. I'm really not sure why I joined."

"Frustration," another said.

"Yes, we want something, but some of us don't really know what it is," said another.

"Mandie, do you think we can really trust her?" the first young woman asked.

"I am positive. Aunt Joan is so loving and understanding. If, for no other reason, she would do it for me. She does not want her heir to get into trouble."

They all thought long and hard.

"Will she bring the angel?" one asked.

"Can she leave him behind? I mean, is she able?" another added.

"She will not bring Lucius," Mandie answered. "He does her bidding. He has always served the Keeper."

"Served the Keeper? We thought that the Keeper served the angel," another chimed in.

"No, not so. He serves her and she can leave him."

It was quiet again. They finally said that they would have to contact other cells as only a very few in each cell knew anyone in the cell on either side of them. Their secrecy seemed elaborate.

"Honey, your memory is excellent," I complimented her.

"It's not really that good, Aunt Joan. I think the Presence enhances it."

She seemed very much in tune with the Presence. How let down she would be after this mission was over and He left her side."

04/22/691 C.R.   After some time Mandie was told that six cells had agreed to hear me. Mandie thought that this was probably almost half their numbers. How wrong she was. I was more frightened than I had ever been in my life. What was I to say to these children? Deep down inside I was even angry at the Emperor and Elaine. Surely they knew that this was beyond my abilities. I was almost frantic.

"Ask the Presence for help, Aunt Joan," Mandie begged me.

"I have, nothing happens," I answered.

"It will though, Aunt Joan, I promise. I know you remember in the ancient writings where it is said of him 'open you mouth wide and I will fill it.' The words, and the courage, come exactly when you need them. It is a simultaneous transfer from Him to you. I promise. You will be spectacular." The meeting was upon us.

Over 500 aspiring rebels came to the meeting using an elaborate plan of approach believing that they would not be detected if they followed their plan. I spoke as I have never spoken before. I assured them that the Emperor was totally benevolent; he wants only good for them; even the most unimportant mortal is of interest to the Emperor and the Immortals; the angels are not there to hurt them unless they hurt someone else; I will represent them to the Immortals, my Governess Elaine, their Metropolitan, the Viceroy, the Emperor; I pledged my honor and my very position to them. One by one, group by group I could see that I was winning most of them over. At one point I was suddenly inspired. I knew by "the Presence" to tell those who did not trust me that they were free to leave without consequence. Those who still had a hostile look began to look around and realized that they were seriously in the minority. Slowly they rose and began to leave, still looking suspicious. I whispered to Lucius whom I knew was nearby and listening to be sure that none of them were apprehended this night. After I was sure that they were gone and had enough time to clear the area, I spoke again.

"Now, my friends, in a few moments I want you to look around. But first I want you to know that the only angel that I brought with me is my personal aide Lucius and he is totally harmless. When I give him leave to become visible, look around, look up. Remember, I brought only Lucius. Now look!"

As they looked around them and upwards, thousands of angels became visible. Some of them gasped and started to panic. I reassured them.

"Remember my promises," I called out. " Not one, not one of them will go unfilled. You are safe. You are pardoned. You never had a chance of hiding. You have always been much loved. Keep calm, children. Keep calm. There is no reason to be frightened or concerned.

"Keeper," one young woman near the front called out. They all fell silent.

"Yes, Me Lu, what is it?"

"You   know   my   name?"

"Yes, and so do the Immortals," I answered confidently. I was not sure how I knew her name. It couldn't have been a lucky guess. It had to be "the Presence;" He had told me. He spoke it to my heart and before I could think and stop myself I spoke it out. It had a wondrous effect. As a result Me Lu trusted me and many others knew it.

"Keeper, many of us are sick in some way or another. Does the Emperor care about this?"

"Yes," another one said. "And we do not have adequate means."

"Why, Kwan Jo, why do you lack adequate means?"

By now many more realized that I had called Kwan Jo by name. The trust level was rising.

"I do not know, Keeper," he responded.

"Because you have not asked for means, for more houses, clothing, or for healing from your Immortals."

"That is all? All we need do is ask?"

"Yes. The Immortals have a charge from the Emperor to help you, but you have not asked. They have been like you are. They can identify with you. They are kind. If they were not, they would not be here. They would still be in their graves. You want to be self sufficient, but you do not need to be. Will you ask now?"

Many nodded. Some cried out, "Yes."

Suddenly Elaine appeared beside me with about 50 other Immortals most of them local and therefore oriental like these mortals.

"My Immortal friends with my Governess Elaine will now pass among you. If you are sick in any way, please tell them and they will fix it. Tell them of your other needs as well," I said.

As the Immortals passed among them wonderful things happened and they began to love each other. There were hugs and even kisses from both mortals and Immortals. Many of them left together. For the following several weeks there were vast crowds at the Dais of the Metropolitan. Groups of mortals and Immortals came and went and the entire area was transformed into a caring community.

Metropolitan Su told me, "Your mission here is a total success, Keeper. And word of it is spreading throughout the entire Principality. We knew that we could not help unless we were asked. Now you have enabled the people to ask."

"Thank you, Metropolitan. I must now go back to the Western side of the world and spread the news."

"Yes. Wonderful. You are truly the Primate." I felt that I was fulfilling what had been an empty title into a blessed reality.

I should add, however, that the rebels that I dismissed were all arrested two days afterwards. They were judged and disciplined by the Metropolitan and others. Those who resisted capture were executed. Both sides of the message were now widely known. The rule is benevolent, but it is a rule, and an absolute one. I felt that most people would choose the benevolence, at least for some time to come.

Before we went home to Henry Sawyer's court we stopped at Patmos to see the Viceroy. Mandie had never met him and I wanted her to have the experience. Patmos was still beautiful and the Viceroy was still the personification of love second only to the Emperor. He took a real interest in Mandie.

"The young Keeper Heiress," John said and he put his arm around her shoulders. Mandie was glowing.

"Yes, Excellency. It is so wonderful to meet you."

"And to meet you, child. Welcome to my Dais. Here, sit next to me, let's talk. You have quite a job ahead of you, young lady." They talked for over three hours that day and met everyday for over two weeks. I busied myself by speaking around the Mediterranean. If I were younger, I might be jealous. But by now I was glad for every minute she got with him.

Mandie and I spent the next four years spreading the news of love on both sides of the world.

11.15.699 C.R. My name is Mandie. I am the new Keeper and Primate. My beloved aunt Joan died last night in her sleep. She labored until the last spreading the news of love. There was not a single day that she did not feel the Presence since she started this work. I long to be her faithful successor.

5 * MERLE

810 - 875 C.R.

12.20.810 C.R.   My name is Merle. I am the thirteenth in the Annatic line and the daughter of Ken. The year of my investiture is 810 C.R. I will state from the beginning that I have one and only one goal in my offices: to establish among mortals the worldwide worship of the Emperor. Like my predecessors since Joan, I am the Keeper of the Ancient Books, the Primary Interpreter of the books of Anna, the Chronicler of Imperial truth, and the Spiritual Primate of the mortals on the earth. My predecessors in their position as Spiritual Primate should have established the worship of the Emperor by now. Since they have not, I will make it my supreme goal. I will not vary from this task for any reason. It was May that first inspired the worship of the Emperor among mortals; she was the most spiritual. Since Joan each Keeper and Primate has favored worship of the Emperor and has encouraged groups which have formed on their own for this purpose. By the wearing of the red belt they have silently proclaimed their office as Spiritual Primate of the mortals on the earth. In this office they should have actively encouraged massive and open worship of the Emperor. The Immortals have their own relationship with the Emperor in the "away" place. They fellowship with Him and worship him there. This is not my concern.

01.04.811 C.R.   My investiture as the Keeper of the Ancient Books, the Primary Interpreter of the books of Anna, and the Spiritual Primate of the mortals on the earth was only two short weeks ago. I am now waiting to learn when the Immortals will invest me with the title of the Chronicler of Imperial truth. This can come at any time, as early as one month after the others and as long as two years. I have asked for a meeting with Elaine to find out how soon it will come. I feel that I can better accomplish my important task with all of the titles, although as Spiritual Primate I can start my campaigns at any time.

01.25.811 C.R.   Lucius prompted me to Elaine's arrival by moving himself directly in front of my face. This is a practice that my father Ken had trained him to do. I was prepared for her arrival. She could have bid me come to her.

"Elaine. Hello."   She had not given me permission to address her in the familiar. Later she told me that my abrupt personality was well known among the Immortals and that they said "the Emperor help any who ignore her."

"You want to know when you will be invested as the Chronicler of Imperial Truth."

I was not surprised that she knew.

"I am told that it will be tomorrow," Elaine said.

I was surprised. This has never been a large or complicated ceremony so it can be done with short notice, but this was very fast.

02.22.811 C.R.   Thanks to the work of my father using his title as Spiritual Primate of the mortals on the earth there are Emissaries from this office in every major city of the world. My father set up this organization in order to collect and distribute information from his office here at the Residence to these Emissaries throughout the mortal world. The existence of this system is, of course, approved by our Governors at every level, and, therefore, I presume by the Emperor Himself. Neither my father nor myself has ever been personally in the presence of the

Emperor. The Immortal Elaine has oversight for all of our work. My mother, Esther, is still with me and we are very close. She has no official position in the Annatic line, but I regard her advice very highly. I propose to use this system that my father established to gather and share information to promote the cause. First, I will instruct my Emissaries to find out where the Emperor is being worshipped and to summarize this knowledge and report it to me. In order to keep people from coming to worship services to receive favor from me or our Immortal governors, I will instruct my Emissaries to gather their information carefully. Then I will begin my campaign to present the Emperor as one worthy of worship and adoration. Every thing that my predecessors and I have learned shows that the Emperor is worthy of admiration as a man and worship as God. He has ruled now for 810 years. The Immortals have their own intensely personal relationship with Him. For generations and centuries we mortals have lived under his benevolent rule. There is no violence, disease, hardship or want of any kind in the world. Mortals that abuse or harm others in any way are immediately dealt with by the angels and the Immortals. My father's research and mine has led me to believe that the Immortals spend less and less time with us every mortal generation. Our mortal magistrates handle minor matters of peace and order. The Immortals spend most of the time "away" with the Emperor in that "next-door-place" where only they can go. Although everything seems to be continually most pleasant, I sense, as my father did, that there is something missing in the mortal world. My father believed that it was to be my mission to change this. I believe that wide spread worship of the Emperor is the answer. We can find our meaning and destiny in Him.

[N.D.]   I believe that the differences in our condition as mortals and the condition of our Immortals when they were mortal should be important. Over the past

800 plus years we of the Annatic line have distilled out a few vital differences. I will begin with the similarities. Both mortal conditions, ours now and theirs before the Glorious return, involve being born with a nature that does not naturally love the Emperor or His Father. They called this nature "sin." We have no established name for it; it has been prominently called "rebellion." When they were mortals, there was an invisible evil angel prince and his many angels and other spirits that worked against the Emperor. Both this evil angel prince and his agents and the Emperor were invisible except for the 33 years when the Emperor came among mortals as a man. Now that evil prince and his minions have been bound away from the world completely and continuously. The greatest thing that our Immortals had when they were mortal was the "Helper." We know Him as the "Presence." Along with the Emperor and His Father He is another form of God who actually lived within mortals who were loyal to the Emperor from the time He came as a man until the Glorious Return. We do not have the "Presence" available to us on a permanent basis, but neither do we have the invisible evil forces to contend with. In rare instances, such as with May and Joan, the "Presence" stays with us to accomplish a specific purpose. I have not yet experienced this; I hope that I will. The angels of the Emperor are now visible to us. They were not visible except by special visions or dreams before the Glorious Return. The Immortals are among us as rulers and judges and, in some cases as Elaine has been with our lineage, as friends. Before the Glorious Return people were "converted" to the Emperor and their inner rebellious self was, as I understand it, largely subdued by the "Helper." We seem to develop our loyalty to the Emperor by observing the greatness and goodness of His rule and learning to be loyal, although there are some who do not grow or develop in this manner. Finally, and perhaps most important, when our Immortals

were mortal and they converted to the Emperor, they were assured of life after death or eternal life in a new but similar body. This they have now as Immortals in our midst. The promise of eternal life for us is not clear. Some mortals believe in it now; some do not.

11.12.813 C.R. I have been receiving information from my Emissaries for over a year now. The mortal Emissaries collect and record the information and Lucius brings the reports to me.

The most disturbing area in these reports are the instances of the worship of angels found throughout the world. Since no visible angel will knowingly receive worship, these meetings are held in secret, but my agents have been successful in penetrating these angel worshipping cells worldwide. It has occurred to me that I myself do not know much about angels. In researching the writings of my predecessors I find many mentions of angels but relatively little about their nature or organization. I retired to my library for several days to research this some more and was disappointed with what I found, or rather what I did not find. We have seen angels all of our lives. Every Immortal Princely Ruler has his or her own retinue of them. Angels appear at the Immortals bidding to transport offenders to the Dais of the ruler. And I, I am the only mortal with an angel of my own; or rather one who has always been with the Keeper over the centuries. As I sat in frustration in my library I glanced up to see Lucius waiting patiently over near the wall to my side. It suddenly occurred to me to ask him some questions. I was not optimistic that he would be much help as he had never been known to have much to say. But I should have known that there was no hard and fast rule on this.

"Lucius," I said, looking up from my books.

He approached and stood in front of me.

I studied him for a minute. He has been with me personally for some time now, but I have seen him all my life as he attended my father. It is strange how we do not really see many of those around us. He had a face that was usual for an angel. His eyes and mouth were well defined. There is a slight protrusion where a human nose would be, but this was not well defined; angels do not breathe. There was also a slight appearance of ears. His overall appearance was one of brightness but this was not as bright as normal daylight on a clear day. In a dark or mostly darkened room, however, the brightness of an angel was very clear. Lucius had arms like all angels; they resembled more the arms of a man than of a woman. He had legs but they were obscured by a haze which resembled a tight skirt. This same haze covered his upper torso as well. There was an additional prominent hazy area between his shoulders in the back. These were not wings as such but they had something to do with his ability to "fly" or transport himself. Lucius' face was distinguishable from other angels merely by the size, shape and arrangement of the features which is similar to humans, but they all tend to resemble each other more than humans do. Like the Immortals they do not show any signs of aging as we mortals do. I realized that I had been studying Lucius for some time. I became slightly self-conscious. His expression did not change. Angels are innately very patient, or something which we would understand as patience. This is probably because they have no doubts whatsoever about the outcome of anything. I do not believe that this is because they know the outcome of everything before its conclusion but merely because they know that the Emperor's will shall always be accomplished and that it is always the best possible outcome. And then, of course, they can not know death. The only angel that I or any of my time have seen thus far that looks much different than Lucius and the other angels is Gabriel. He is very much taller than the others and has a massive head. His eyes are large and piercing. He is obviously quite special. Gabriel always leads the Emperor's own cortège.

Lucius had made no response to my staring. This was predictable.

"Lucius, how many angels are there?" I asked.

"More than can be numbered, Keeper."

"O come now, Lucius, anything can be numbered," I objected.

"Not angels, Keeper, not by you or by myself."

So far I was not learning much.

"Lucius," This time I was raising my voice. I surprised myself with the volume.

"How many kinds of angels are there?"

"Nine, Keeper. Three Hierarchies of three Ranks each."

Now that was specific.

"How are they called," I asked still somewhat loudly. My librarian came scurrying in my direction looking somewhat surprised and, yes, even stern.

"Do you, er . . ., need something, Keeper?" She asked.

"No, nothing. Nothing from you," I said and motioned for her to go away. I was excited that Lucius was answering so well. She withdrew slowly with a pouting look on her face. "This is my library," I shouted after her. Surprised she cast her eyes down and backed away. Janine was a good librarian and had been my father's for over 20 years. She was not quite used to me being the Keeper and she has always kept others quiet in the library with her stern demeanor including me as a child. I did not expect any more attitude from her.

Lucius continued his answer. "The High-Hierarchy consists of the Seraphs,
Cherubs and Worshippers Ranks, Keeper."

"And   the   next?"

"The Mid-Hierarchy."

"Mid-Hierarchy, yes, what is there?"

"The Mid-Hierarchy consists of the Princes, Vicars and Chiefs Ranks."

"Then what?" I asked.

"The Low-Hierarchy, Keeper. It consists of the Archangels, Heralds, and Angels Ranks."

He then stood silent again. I assumed that I could get the information I needed if he knew the answers and if I asked enough questions. I had picked up a pen and was writing all this down.

"So then, which Ranks within the Hierarchies are the highest?"

"Keeper?"

"Well, for instance, the Archangels are the highest of the Low-Hierarchy?"

"Yes, Keeper."

"And the Princes, the highest in the Mid-Hierarchy?"

"Yes, Keeper. And the Seraphs, the highest of the highest." He finished it.

"What Rank are you from, Lucius?"

"I am an angel. We are divided into lower divisions called Legions."

I counted myself blessed to have one of the lowest to help me.

"And Gabriel?"

"He is a Herald."

"And Michael?"

"He is an Archangel."

"What is the highest ranking angel seen on earth by mortals, Lucius?"

"The Lord, Michael." He answered in his usual unemotional manner.

"Then what, what do the other - what is it?- the other five Ranks do?"

"They serve the Emperor elsewhere, Keeper."

"Elsewhere as in the 'next-door-place' er, beyond the veil?" I asked.

"Yes."

"How?"

"The High-Hierarchy attends only the Emperor and His Father beyond the veil."

"That is the Seraphs, Cherubs and Worshippers Ranks?"

"Yes."

"What about the top two Ranks in the Mid-Hierarchy?" I asked.

"The Princes and Vicars?."

"Yes, we do not see them but they do not attend only the Emperor and His Father beyond the veil," I said.

"Yes." Lucius answered.

"What do they do?" I insisted.

"They rule and influence here and elsewhere, Keeper."

"Rule and influence?"

"Yes, the Princes rule on other worlds. The Vicars influence for good behind the scenes in many places."

Somehow, that seemed to make sense. "Do you know the names of other angels? Higher ones like Princes or Vicars?" I asked.

"Yes, Keeper."

"What are some of them, Lucius?"

"One is Raphael."

"Raphael I have heard of, "I answered.

"He proclaims God's healing," Lucius answered.

"And Michael, what does he, . . .do?"

"He asks, who is like God?" Lucius answered bowing at the name of God. "He has always protected the Emperor's natural relatives."

Either I had exhausted his knowledge of his own kind or he did not intend to tell me more. I pushed a little farther. "Are there any more important ones?" I asked.

"One, Keeper. At least he was."

"His name?"

"Lucifer. He is important no longer. He is bound in chains with those who followed him." Lucius almost seemed happy.

"I know of him in the ancient writings. What rank was he?"

"He was a Cherub, Keeper, but the only one of his kind. He was the living veil over the face of God."

"So high! And he rebelled?"

"Yes, Keeper, very high. He did rebel."

"Did they follow him from all Ranks?"

"Most Ranks, Keeper."

"Have you seen Seraphs, Lucius?" I asked.

"Yes, on the day we all were made, I saw," He answered.

"So, all angels, like people were created by God," I said just for clarity.

"Yes, Keeper."

Again for clarity, "Except the Emperor."

"Except the Emperor," he bowed again.

"Heralds, Lucius. Do I know any?"

"You know the leader of the Metropolitan's escort."

"Metropolitan Henry, our Metropolitan?"

"Yes, Keeper. Dexter is the head of his escort. He stands behind the
Metropolitan always at the Dais and goes before him when he moves."

"Yes, Dexter. I have heard him called this. He looks like you and the
other angels."

"Yes. All within each Rank look alike. Except for some facial features,
of course."

I thought. They can tell the difference in facial features of angels better than

178

humans can. Still again, Dexter did have a certain glow of benign authority that the others around the Metropolitan's Dais did not. With that I decided to quit for now. "Thank you, Lucius." He returned to his place by the wall.

[N.D.] I have decided to issue a proclamation.

"To all mortals upon the earth from Merle, the thirteenth in the Annatic line, the daughter of Ken, the Keeper of the Ancient Books, the Primary Interpreter of the books of Anna, the Chronicler of Imperial truth, and the Spiritual Primate of the mortals on the earth. Hear what I have to say my brothers and sisters. It has been brought to my attention that some are worshipping angels in secret meetings throughout the earth. This is very bad and it must stop. Angels of every rank are created beings just like all people. I am petitioning both Viceroys to assign angels to search out these meetings and put an end to them. The only Person worthy of worship in this world is the Emperor Himself. Be attentive and obey. Punishment awaits those who do not obey."

This gave me an excellent opportunity to encourage the worship of the Emperor. After I finished writing, I gave the proclamation to Lucius and told him to take it to Elaine for approval. I did not include what I had learned from Lucius. My father had always said that partial knowledge about mysteries usually leads to wrongdoing. I will put that in my private journal. My line has always kept a private journal since May. She was so devout and knew so much that she had to separate her journals.

[N.D.] The next morning after I awoke Lucius told me that Elaine would arrive in one hour and that I was to accompany her to the court of the Viceroy of the Western hemisphere, Luis Cepata in Montevideo. I wondered if I had overstepped my bounds. "Oh, no, dear Merle," Elaine said. "Quite the contrary. You have done really well." She gave me a quick hug. I was deeply touched. I do not remember her ever hugging my father although Anna and Joan and May reported such things in their private diaries.

"Are you ready to leave?" she asked me.

"Yes, yes of course."

"Good, my escort is arriving here. First, let me tell you a few things about the Viceroy."

I reached for my notebook, but she signaled me to leave it.

"Luis Cepata was martyred less than a year before the return of the Emperor. Many of us wondered why he should be given the only position equal to John the Beloved, but we have learned not to question the Emperor's decisions."

"But Immortals can't rebel," I blurted.

"You are correct. Jealousy and its cousins are no longer in us, but we are still human. So sometimes we are perplexed about the Emperor's decisions at least until we meet him in the family setting behind the veil."

"Then you understand?"

"Not necessarily, but then, we don't care. I have said that to Keepers before."

"It must be wonderful there."

"Yes, yes it is. Back to the Viceroy."

I gave her my undivided attention.

"Luis was born in renewal and he knew nothing else his entire life. His country was dominated by the renewal that only the Helper could bring. At a fairly young age he became President of his country and he ruled in a very just and compassionate manner always encouraging others below him to do the same."

Elaine had not briefed me before; so I paid special attention. I could remember only two or three occasions on which she had briefed my father. Maybe there had been more as I was not always with him.

She sat down and motioned me to sit beside her. Then she continued, "Luis gave daily testimony to the Emperor and prayed publicly many times that his life and rule would reflect the Emperor. Then his country was invaded by an evil government from a nation nearby and Luis was taken captive. He surrendered himself willingly over the advice of his aides. I don't think he believed that they would actually mistreat him. But even if he had believed it, he would have wanted to give witness to the Emperor to these invaders. He lived about three months in their prison and they treated him very badly. His last words were words of praise to the Emperor. This infuriated his captors. Upon his return the first two Dais' that the Emperor awarded were to John the Beloved and Luis Cepata, the two Viceroys. Well, now let's go."

I did not have a chance to say anything before Elaine lifted her scepter and a portal formed and we found ourselves at the Dais in Montevideo. For a fleeting second I thought I was aware of us passing through a bright hall and Elaine waving to some other Immortals through a wide doorway in an adjoining room, but it was fleeting, very fleeting, and I did not really think about it until I went to bed that night.

[N.D.] The Dais in Montevideo was, as usual, on the top of a mountain overlooking the country. The seats were set up the same as those at Patmos, much grander than a Metropolitan's court or the court of a regional Prince such as Janice. The view was magnificent. The Viceroy was a short man, shorter than myself and I was considerably shorted than Elaine. He had a dark complexion and thick black hair in line with his Latino heritage. He had an infectious smile and he stood as we arrived. I knew that he did not stand for me. It must have been out of courtesy for Elaine as Imperial Legate. He had apparently been in the midst of a judgment as two mortals were taken to one side and held by an angel.

"Welcome, welcome Elaine." The Viceroy hugged Elaine then turned to me.

"And welcome Merle, welcome Keeper, congratulations on your appointment."

"Thank you, Excellency."

Elaine's escort took their place behind the Viceroy's and was all but lost. The angelic canopy here was as magnificent as the one at Patmos. However, I sensed more of a Latin flavor in the tones emanating from this canopy than at Patmos. I thought this somewhat odd as the angels were not Latin, but then I remembered that it was the Viceroy's pleasure that would be accommodated here. I smiled at this; everything in the Kingdom was so appropriate. Elaine motioned for me to sit at her side as she sat near the Viceroy. There was still the empty seat for the Emperor. Some mortal brought a stool for me. I remembered from her journals that Anna herself had to sit on the grass beside Elaine. The weight of my responsibilities seemed strong on me.

Cepata turned again to the judgment before him. The men were brought forth.

"You have been charged with insurrection," an Immortal prosecutor announced.

"How could you ever have dreamed that you could overthrow the Emperor?" Cepata asked.

They stood silent and defiant.

"You will answer the Viceroy," the prosecutor said.

Finally, one of them said, "We want responses for injustice from the Emperor."

"What injustices?" Cepata asked.

"For one thing, we are not allowed to elect our own rulers, the ones we are allowed to elect have no real power," the other added.

"This is not the time of elections. This is the time of the Sovereign Kingdom," the Viceroy said.

"We have read the histories. You were elected 'el Presidente' when you were mortal." the second one countered.

I thought that he had some nerve.

"That era is past. The Emperor has returned. You are not mistreated. There is no need among you. Why do you plan such things and attempt to recruit an army. In the first place you could not win. You are very foolish and rebellious," the Viceroy affirmed.

They stood defiant.

"I will show you," Cepata said determined. I felt a flash of fear myself.

The angels were commanded to assemble every member of the would-be rebel forces in the valley before us. This took several minutes. It was announced that there were 3,871 people in the rebel group who had vigorously attended planning meetings. Their two leaders looked down from the Dais.

"See this!" the Viceroy said as he raised his scepter and announced, "I am Luis Cepata, Viceroy of the Western Hemisphere under the Imperial Righteous Rule of the Emperor in Jerusalem." He swept his scepter across the valley before him. Instantly the little army of rebels before him disappeared. The two leaders fell to their knees in shock prepared to die.

"You will now go back and tell all you know of what has happened here," the Viceroy commanded.

"Yes, Majesty," the most rebellious one muttered.

"Not, Majesty," the Viceroy corrected, "your Highness will do, I am a Prince, not the Emperor."

"Yes, Highness."

"These two angels will watch you constantly." Two angels came forth for this guard duty. The men were surprised that they were to be allowed to live, at least for now. The angels took them by the arm and they were gone.

"Is the rebel force dead?" I whispered to Elaine.

She shook her head, 'No.'

"Now I have a task for the Keeper," Cepata said. "We have many beautiful Cathedrals here. They were used in times past for the worship of the Emperor. Since the Return the Dais has been the spiritual and political center of each area. Your proclamation encouraging the worship of the Emperor by mortals in these days was inspiring." He paused.

"Thank you, Viceroy," I responded.

"Now these buildings are being used for a variety of things: museums, civic centers, theaters, and such. I will issue an order in my hemisphere that they all be returned to their original use, that of worship of the Emperor. Granted, you do not live in the age of grace and faith. The Emperor is here. But such worship will be good for all mortals. We Immortals have our time with Him. Perhaps He will even visit these cathedrals after this is instituted. Angels will be assigned to these places. You have made it clear that they are not to be worshipped and they will echo your message. Incorrect images will be removed from these places and other buildings will be found or built if necessary to accommodate their present uses. The people will lose nothing. It will all be blessing and gain. I want you to supervise the undertaking and schedule the worship times. I will assign you extra angels. Your Lucius can guide them as you see fit. What do you say?"

"Viceroy, I am overwhelmed. It is wonderful."

"And, and," the Viceroy added excitedly, "I talked to John the Beloved at the last Imperial dinner and he said that he will do the same in his realm." The Viceroy literally beamed at the prospect.

I was truly overwhelmed. I had expected my task to be long and hard. Now with the involvement of the two Viceroys it would proceed very quickly.

"Very good, Elaine," Cepata said smiling at Elaine. "We should now make your position as Imperial Legate public. Your appearances at these sites will encourage everyone and still leave the actual impetus in the hands of the Keeper." Elaine nodded in agreement. It suddenly occurred to me that they had shown much patience in waiting for my line to move to bring this about. It was, I now realize, probably one of their primary objectives in establishing the entire Annatic dynasty. If the Immortals were so strange in their natures and actions to us, I wondered if we could ever understand the Emperor himself.

09.12.821 C.R. I have accomplished much in the comparatively short time that I have been in office. Today is my 32nd birthday. I have been so zealous to see the establishment of the worship of the Emperor that I have had no private life. Today Elaine informed me that she has identified my future husband. According to the journals Elaine has not always taken this direct approach. It has varied depending upon the personality of the Keeper. Evidently I require the direct approach. I do not mind because I would not have the slightest idea how to pick a mate. I have never thought of myself as particularly attractive. I have red hair and I have always been a little overweight even as a child. I have always felt awkward around men and I have always used my position as the future Keeper and then as Keeper to shield me from having to relate to men. I believe that I have normal desires and drives, but I have always lived a privileged life so I have just let my duties be everything to me. If Elaine wants me to marry and bear a successor, then I will do so. I am sure that it is not merely because the Immortals are so fond of weddings. I will try to like and even to love the man who has been chosen for me. But I would rather give a thousand speeches than meet him tomorrow.

02.12.822 C.R.   Elaine told me to come to her residence. Lucius took me to her reception parlor. We greeted, hugged and sat down to drinks.

At my very first sight of Andre I was at ease. We must be soul mates. He is mature, a little older than I. He is taller than I am but not too tall. He has blond hair and almost chiseled masculine features and a wonderful smile. He acts like he already loves me. Has he been watching me from afar? At least I know that he is not an opportunity seeker as he could not fool the Immortals. I was afraid I would be speechless when we met, so I had rehearsed several lines which I promptly forgot. I did not need them.

I must admit that the Immortals in their wisdom have the ability to choose the perfect mate. I know that they themselves do not mate or bear children as they did when they were mortals. But they have vast experience in this as mortals and they always remember every detail of their mortal lives. Elaine says that her memory as an Immortal is perfect regarding everything she has experienced both as a mortal and an Immortal. She says that she did not remember as well when she was a mortal. I suppose that these memories are what enable them to choose a mate for me so expertly.

02.29.822 C.R.   Andre is a most attentive man. His goal in life seems to be to support me in my duties as Keeper and to encourage and nurture me personally. He is gentle, yet strong. He is happy, yet efficient. He adores me and I love him for it. I was a little nervous as our wedding night approached but he put me at ease at every stage. And, of course, the wedding itself was managed by Elaine herself and was a wonderful affair. As usual with every Keeper except Joan who did not marry, the Over-Lord Janice or the Metropolitan or both of them perform the marriage ceremony. Both of them performed mine.

10.01.822 C.R.   I was married today at the age of 33 years. Being somewhat old for a bride and constantly battling with my weight made me a nervous bride. But everyone involved strived to make it easier for me. Elaine had a dress made that made me look at least twenty pounds lighter except in the chest where Andre said it "counts the most." I felt like the original Earth Mother. The ceremony was magnificent with full escorts and thousands of mortal guests and five entire escorts of angels between Elaine, the Metropolitan and the Over-Lord plus both Viceroys sent representatives who also had escorts. Elaine is the direct representative of the Emperor as Imperial Legate. Lucius quickly whisked us away to our island wedding trip after the reception was over and then he conveniently placed himself in another room of our suite for a couple of days.

[N.D.] I am surprised by love. We have been on our wedding trip for almost two weeks now. I never imagined that it could be so wonderful. Andre is a wonderful lover and we are already best friends. I have no desire to return to my duties, but I know that I shall have to very soon.

[N.D.]   At first I was concerned that Andre would be bored while I was at work but this has not been a problem. He has set up a desk next to me. He has assured me that I am the Keeper but he is my willing assistant and advisor. He says that when he makes mistakes that Elaine will catch them as surely as she does mine. Work flies by with two of us working, and that leaves room for plenty of private life, something that is a continual delight to me and to Andre. I hope I shall conceive a child soon.

04.12.828 C.R.   The first six years of our married life were consumed with establishing worship centers throughout the world. We visited everywhere. In each place these buildings were cleaned and repaired and restored. The very presence of a few angels in each building brightened them considerably. The angels showed their ability to generate more light. Worship services were scheduled and planned by me. Mortal printers under contract to the government printed and distributed the materials.

Many of these ancient Cathedrals were immense. I thought that candle light was an appropriate addition to the angelic glow. Our usual electric lighting seemed so mundane. Whole companies were created to make and distribute candles. Since there was an aroma around our Immortals when they returned from the presence of the Emperor, I ordered that the candles be scented. I instructed Lucius to supply several appropriate aromas and to show the candle makers how to produce them. The candles should also be colored to go with the aromas. I started to hold auditions in each Cathedral for musicians and singers.

It was not long before it was obvious that I would need help. The angels could get the word out and gather those who were interested, but I would need mortals to audition and lead the orchestras and ranks. So I began to interview and audition potential leaders and assign them to assemble and rehearse the orchestras and ranks. I issued guidelines for all of these activities. The musicians asked for the appropriate words to be coupled with their music of praise to the Emperor. I was frantic as I thought about interviewing poets and writers from among the populace when I remembered something from the ancient books. An ancient king of Israel, King David, and some others had written 150 songs of praise to the Emperor and His Father. I had these words distributed to be used in these songs of praise.

People began to meet in these beautiful buildings to sing praises to The Emperor and His Father. If any area lacked a building, the Viceroy would order one built. Every effort was taken to make the new buildings resemble the old ones. In my research I had been surprised at the different beliefs about the Emperor that existed. After a while I realized that the people should not only sing but they should also repeat certain beliefs about the Emperor. I remembered that these had been called "Creeds" in ancient times. So I rewrote some of these for our use. I also recruited scholars, men and women of honor from among us, to give lessons about the Emperor both from the past and the present using materials from my library. Janine suddenly got very, very busy. All of this was a tremendous undertaking. But it seemed popular among mortals and was very exciting to the Immortals. No one resisted these activities. These services were held twice a week in most locations. Fortunes were made in the candle industry and the printing industry and the building industry and many others as a result of these activities. This will have to be investigated.

07.12.840 C.R.   As the worship services began to be held world wide, there was one surprising thing that emerged. I had stationed a certain number of angels at each cathedral as guardians and providers of that kind of light that only they can generate. To the surprise of everybody the angels joined enthusiastically in the actual worship experience. They harmonized with the chords in the songs, raised their arms, danced in the air and actually shouted at times, appropriate times. Before long other angels arrived and joined in as well. At first the mortals tended to be frightened. My speakers assured them that no harm would come from the angels. The numbers of angels at the services was soon greater than the number of mortals. A few Immortals came to observe and joined in the worship. But they have their own services beyond the veil. Finally I had to limit the number of angels at the services to 10,000 for each cathedral. Even this is only possible because the angels do not use any chairs or floor space. They hover on the upper walls and the ceiling. They take so naturally to this activity that I did not want to limit their attendance but it was necessary. As affirmed by William to my great grandmother Joan, the myriads of angels are almost without number. At our gatherings there have also been seen significant numbers of the Mid-Hierarchy of angels, the larger ones with the large heads and piercing eyes. They look more like Gabriel since he belongs to the Chiefs Rank in that Hierarchy. We suspect that some of the ones seen at the gatherings may even be from the Princes Rank. I do not expect the High-Hierarchy to appear on this side of the veil. The participation of the angels made the voluntary attendance of mortals at these gatherings grow tremendously. Where else except at a Viceroy's canopy could such a demonstration of angels be seen? Most mortals have not seen a Viceroy's canopy, so these services were very popular. The Immortals were even more pleased. And I was even more praised. I made definite efforts to see that Andre's help received proper appreciation, although he does not seem to care.

01.22.843 C.R.   I have now encountered the biggest problem since I have been in office. I am thankful to the Emperor that Andre is by my side to help me deal with it. I have been accused by the civil magistrate of using my position wrongly in order to promote the worship of the Emperor. I have even been accused of using angels to coerce mortals to participate in the services worshiping the Emperor. This comes at a time when we had hoped to slow down and I would be able to conceive an heir. Now we are both quite upset. We have asked for a meeting with Elaine.

"Can't you just have some angels proclaim that these things are not so?" Andre asked.

"I could," Elaine answered. "But those who have brought these charges are basically rebellious. And as you both have learned, anytime that something like this arises the Emperor is always interested to know the complete extent of the rebellion."

We both nodded.

"What is the best course," I asked. "One that will best serve the Emperor?"

"That's my Merle," Elaine said. "You know that as Imperial Legate I can always step in and pronounce you exonerated and arrest those who have been accusing you. We have absolutely no concern for our reputations or the security of the Empire. We have absolute authority from the Emperor and there is no amount of resistance that can overthrow the Emperor. Everything that happens is only to prove the character of human nature."

"I understand."

"The best course is for you to voluntarily subject yourself to the civil court and let it play itself out."

"But what about the authority of my office as Spiritual Primate?"

"You will have to secund this office to someone else until this is over."

"But who? There is no other mortal trained in my positions and Andre is also accused."

"Request that the Viceroys personally hold this responsibility until you are cleared."

"Will I be cleared?"

"One way or the other."

"What does that mean?"

"Either the mortal high court will eventually clear you, or if they fail, the Emperor will order you cleared against their judgment."

"That will leave them in a state of rebellion against the Emperor."

"Precisely."

Andre and I smiled at each other and nodded again.

"Now Merle," Elaine continued, "This does not mean that this will be easy for you, but I will stay nearby to help and encourage both of you. And you will not forfeit Lucius, he will remain and appear with you everywhere."

"Do you think that will be all right?"

"Yes, it will be fine."

09.22.843 C.R.   I wrote letters to the Viceroys. Elaine reviewed them and Lucius was sent to deliver them. Both of them responded within hours. They would hold my office as Spiritual Primate until this affair is over. I wrote to the regional court and agreed to appear. I had this delivered by a mortal member of my staff.

03.23.844 C.R.   My appearance before the mortal regional court was most difficult. Judge Cummings is a little man in every way except girth. We were required to stand as he entered. There were three magistrates for the prosecution. We represented ourselves. I was charged with abuse of my offices in "requiring" people to attend Emperor worship. This was untrue on its face. We made our case citing my proclamations and excerpts from my speeches to the contrary. I stated that I would support an order from the Emperor in this regard, but that I did not personally believe that I had such authority. I was charged with profiteering in regard to things used in Emperor worship, particularly candles. Candles! Even now I can scarcely believe it. I was ordered to present all my personal financial records. I agreed to present certain totals, not every specific. I was summarily found guilty. Sentence was postponed due to my appeal to the appeals court.

04.26.844 C.R.   The appeals court was no better. There were three judges. Each one worse than the other. It upheld the findings of the regional court and added a charge of contempt of court because I had refused to present all my financial records. I objected and a second charge of contempt was added. I appealed to the mortal high court.

05.02.844 C.R.   Winthrop Surratt was the mortal high justice of the Western division of the mortal secular magistrate. He sat in the seat of those who had judged many mortal matters since the time of Mark. He sat at a very high desk so those who were brought before him were forced to look up at him. I was brought before him. He addressed me by Andre's family name.

"Mrs. Jamison, you have been convicted of abuse of your office in all of your titles and profiting from the sale of articles used in cathedral worship by the regional court. The appeals court has upheld these charges and added contempt of court for the entire magisterial system." He paused. "I now uphold both of these courts and find you guilty of all charges." He glared down at me.

I looked back silently. The court was filled with thousands of people, some of them for me, but most of them wanting to see my downfall.

"You have nothing to say?" he asked.

I did not answer.

"You are, therefore, commanded to give up your offices and residences and, along with your husband, find useful and honest employment. You will be on probation under this court for a period of 6 years. You will report . . ."

Before he finished there was a very loud crack as if someone had just broken down a wall. Two enormous angels appeared on each side of the justice. The entire ceiling of the court was packed with an angelic escort usually reserved for an Over-Lord.

"I am Gabriel," one of the great angels said.

"I am Raphael," the other one said.

They each took the Justice by an arm and lifted him out of his chair and up so far that his feet could not touch the floor. He look terrified and perplexed as if he had never imagined that he could be treated this way.

Raphael spoke, " This conviction is set aside by the Emperor. The Keeper is exonerated. This man is condemned. Everyone go to your homes and await proclamations from your Immortal rulers." Then all the angels and the justice and his staff were gone. None of these mortals were ever seen or heard from again.

Lucius moved down quickly and took me and Andre back to the residence.

Every Immortal Prince, Metropolitan, Over-Lord and the two Viceroys proclaimed martial law within the hour. The mortal magistrate was abolished and its buildings were destroyed. Every mortal judge and his family disappeared. I was proclaimed a faithful servant of the Emperor, my office as Spiritual Primate was returned and my proclamations were given the force of Imperial edicts.

05.12.844 C.R.   Strangely enough most of the mortals of the earth did not offer any objection to the imposition of martial law or my exoneration. They simply went back to their daily lives. The Immortal rulers went back to hearing any cases that had been heard by the mortal courts. Rulers below the Metropolitan level were appointed judges as they had been just after the glorious return. The great experiment of trusting mortals to be judges had failed.

"I don't think the Emperor was surprised," Andre said.

"Neither do I," I answered as we rested back at the residence with Elaine. "He proves everyone under His sovereignty. And . . . I love it. I love Him."

Andre agreed and Elaine smiled.

Raphael was not seen again among mortals. As far as anyone, Immortal or mortal, knew this was his first and only appearance among mortals.

[N.D.] It has been some years now since Andre and I married. We have longed for a child and have done everything we can to conceive. Andre has called me "little mother" since the second year of our marriage. Not long after that I started calling him "Daddy." Of course, this has only been in private, just two of the love names that we have for each other. We continued these names when I passed the age of child bearing. We have considered adoption. It is not just that we want an heir for my offices, we also long to be parents, to bring a little one to maturity in the world. Elaine has never questioned us on this. I am going to talk to her today about finding a child to adopt.

"We do so want a child," I said.

"I understand, Merle. It is natural and you will need an heir eventually," Elaine answered. "But I am not sure that adoption is the right way."

"Then how? I am 66 years old." I was wondering since she looks eternally 33 does she forget our mortality and the age of conception.

"I can, . . . arrange for you to bear your own child," she said.

"You can?" . . . I did not yet understand.

"May I?" She extended her hand towards my stomach.

"Uh huh, of course." I responded.

She put one hand on my stomach and the other on my back at the waist and closed her eyes. It grew very quiet and I felt very peaceful. I don't think I actually passed out, I just lost an awareness of the passing of time or of Elaine's touch. When I came to myself, I felt fine. I felt strong. Elaine was holding my hands in hers.

"You have been faithful, dear. And so has Andre. Tell him that you are now fully ready to conceive. If he is concerned about your physical safety in this, and he will be, just tell him that I have strengthened your body to carry and bear this child. You will be fine and so will the child. It will be a daughter."

We sat together for a while. I was so thankful. Not just at the possibility of the child but also as a mortal to have Elaine as a close personal friend. Every Keeper has loved her and felt loved by her.

[N.D.] Andre was very happy and planned several romantic meals for us during the next two weeks. I was soon convinced that I was pregnant. The child was very easy to carry. One young mother at our birthing classes who is 23 years old says that I am having an easier time than she is. She is amazed at my vitality.

[N.D.] Kathryn is beautiful. Andre had her room ready when she arrived; all fixed for a girl. She was born in 856 C.R. when I was 67 years of age. We have been married for 34 years. If I am still alive when she is twenty, I will be 87 then. I will abdicate in her favor.

[N.D.] My Emissaries report that over the past two years millions have responded and gathered to worship the Emperor. Lucius has used the angels provided by the

Viceroys to help. I meet with Elaine regularly. She seems to mostly listen to me. She seems very happy.

[N.D.] I have decided to use the majority of my time in my mature years to raising Kathryn and to finding remote peoples throughout the earth who need to know more about the Emperor. I commissioned Lucius to reference the angelic Legion's vault and prepare a report for me of the most remote peoples of the earth. I set the parameters so that they would find the people groups who are cut off from regular communication with a Dais. To my surprise he found just over 1,000 people groups with a population of 99 or more mortals that were so isolated. I have asked for volunteers who are well informed about the Emperor to come to a new school that I am starting where their knowledge of the Emperor will be tested and improved so that they can relocate to these people groups and teach them everything that they know about the Emperor. They will be my "Special Emissaries," or, more exactly, "The Special Emissaries Of The Keeper Of The Ancient Books, The Primary Interpreter Of The Books Of Anna, The Chronicler Of Imperial Truth, And The Spiritual Primate Of The Mortals On The Earth For The Dissemination Of Information About His Imperial Majesty Who Reigns From Jerusalem To The Unreached Peoples Of The Earth." In plain speech it means that I am reviving the office of "Missionaries" for duties during the Reign.

[N.D.] Today our first group of students has arrived. All volunteers from every area were screened by my regular Emissaries and only the top three out of every hundred were forwarded to me and to my school. I will personally teach ten classes of 100 students with the assistance of Andre, my three senior librarians, Lucius and even Elaine. After we are satisfied that they have enough training, Elaine will arrange for their Commencement ceremony at the Dais of the appropriate Viceroy. Then they will be taken with some necessary supplies to their fields of work within that Viceroyage by an angel and left there. This work will take years. Carrie is the most promising student of my first class. She is absolutely devoted.

06.17.875 C.R. My name is Kathryn. Mother died in her sleep last night. We never seem to get used to our mortality. Elaine woke me with the news. In a way Elaine is as close to me as mother was. In the past few years mother put most of her time and energy into her new school which has developed wonderfully. I know I will miss mother, but now I am busy with the memorial plans. She will be buried here at the residence as all the Keepers have been since Anna herself. Then I must prepare to continue her work. The Emperor be praised!

6 * TIM

948 – 999 C.R.

05.05.948 C.R. I was in a deep sleep after a long and difficult evening. I had substituted for my Aunt Kathryn at the Dais reception. The Metropolitan holds a reception twice a year at the Dais for many of the mortal leaders in his principality and from time to time he will give an award for outstanding community service to some deserving mortal. Aunt Kathryn was not feeling well the day of the reception so she went back to the residence and asked me to substitute for her. If she had asked Elaine for help, she could have been healed but she did not choose to do so. Since I have been her understudy for over a year now, it was not thought unusual when I took her place. I presented the outstanding subject for his award and the Metropolitan was, as usual, very congenial in presenting it. It was a way to involve mortals in the leadership of the community and to keep down any unrest that might be tempted to raise its ugly head.

At first I was not aware what had awakened me. The crickets and night birds were still chirping softly under the half moon over the surrounding park and meadows. Then I noticed that Lucius was in my room. This could only mean one thing. Aunt Kathryn had died. I made my way to the reception room and was crossing it to Aunt Kathryn's bedroom when a portal opened and Elaine arrived.

"Bless your heart, Tim. I had not expected it," Elaine said taking my arm.

I squeezed her hand and we went into Aunt Kathryn's room. She looked like she was still sleeping. Lucius was always with her and he knew immediately when she departed. He went directly to tell Elaine and then came to my side. I like Lucius very much, but I will have to get used to his constant presence. Before long many mortal officials and friends arrived and Aunt Kathryn's body was removed for preparation for the memorial service.

05.07.948 C.R. My name is Tim. I am the 15th generation from Mother Anna by direct succession. It is the year 948 C.R., almost a thousand years of the Emperor's reign. When I was born, it was expected within the Annatic family that I would be her spiritual heir. I was born late in the 14th generation and the Immortals had not shown favor on any of the other children. Elaine herself, still vice-regent of Atlanta, is still our family's overseer. She had always favored one child in each generation since Anna. Kathryn, my aunt, has raised me as my mother Elizabeth died in childbirth. It was generally believed that I was the hope of the family. Elaine confirmed this before I was 2 years old. I was allowed free access on a first name basis to Elaine and her household from the time I could walk. I walked in the same favor that Anna had enjoyed. I am the Keeper of the Ancient Books, the Primary Interpreter of the books of Anna, the Chronicler of Imperial truth, and the Spiritual Primate of the mortals on the earth. I was recognized as the Keeper and Primary Interpreter of the ancient books and as the Spiritual Primate at the age of 20. The title of Chronicler of Imperial Truth can only be bestowed by the Immortals. They bestowed it two years later when I was 22.

09.19.948 C.R. Today I have just finished entering the dates for the beginning of office as Keeper and the date of death for each of my predecessors in the public and private journals. I feel that this is appropriate and helpful for any who may read them as it will provide a context for the services of all the Keepers during the Glorious Reign of the Emperor. I began in 948 C.R. at the age of 18. I must admit that I am curious about the end. What will happen by the year 1,000 C.R.? I will be 69 years of age then.

10.01.948 C.R.   My investiture as the Chronicler of Imperial Truth was quite an affair. It was held at the court of the Over-Lord Janice and the Metropolitan and Elaine were there with full ceremonial escorts. Janice's own escort turned out for the event even though it was at her home Dais. There were some visitors from other principalities, but they were not the chief princes like the Metropolitan. The Immortal council assembled and overran the Dais. Thousands of mortals where assembled facing the Dais. I walked down the center aisle just behind Elaine with Lucius just over my head. Everyone mortal or Immortal was standing. When I arrived at the Dais, Janice put the cord of office for the Chronicler around my neck and proclaimed my offices. The Immortals clapped and the mortals cheered. Just as Janice was stepping back and about to bid everyone sit for my acceptance remarks, an unprecedented thing happened. A very large angel appeared at Janice's side. Janice turned and nodded respectfully.

"We are honored to have Gabriel, at our court," she said. "You have something for us?"

The immense angel nodded. His head seemed very large today. He stands at nearly 8 feet and the Over-Lord Janice is so tiny. But height is not the measure of authority. He would have followed any instruction that Janice had given him so long as it did not disrespect the Emperor. He is respected as one of the great angels created with a total freedom of the will just like a human. Another is Michael and another is imprisoned during this Reign for the crime of rebellion against the Emperor and His Father. Also, Gabriel is respected because he speaks for the Emperor.

Janice gestured at the angel. He spoke directly to me in a normal conversational volume.

"The Emperor bids you well, Tim, son of Anna. He wishes you to know that your work is very important to Him and to the Empire. Be diligent, be faithful, be true. Your efforts will not be forgotten."

I was overwhelmed. Why me? This had never happened to any of my predecessors. I was quiet for several seconds at the Dais. As I remained speechless, I looked to Janice. She thanked the angel who stood to one side and remained with us. She bid me bring my acceptance remarks. Fortunately, I had memorized them. I believe that I did a credible job of delivering them.. Afterward Janice praised the Glorious Name of the Emperor and everyone was dismissed to share and to visit. Gabriel then blinked out of sight. I have always wondered at this unusual event, but it has also been proven to be a source of strength and encouragement to me during difficult times.

[N.D.] Mark's blue matrimonial robe looks somewhat worn now. It is over eight hundred years old. It is frayed on the white edges and I have long since quit wearing Joan's red belt. I do not have the recognition that Joan had. I still wear the robe in my annual report to the Over-Lord. This is my day to give my fifth report. I have had the old robe carefully cleaned and mended again. I can not imagine what else I could wear for my annual report. Elaine arrived right on time and along with Lucius and her entourage we went to the Over-Lord's Dais. Janice is as delightful as ever and looks no different than I have ever seen her or as Anna described her.

She accepted my report immediately which consisted mostly with a review of my studies and publication for the past year. I am not a very original writer but I try to keep a variety of works before the public either by republishing some of my predecessors works or presenting them in summary form. I am pretty good at summaries. I also publish a devotional guide each month and make it readily available. I try to avoid reporting on the responses to my work. There are always a faithful few who will say what the work has meant to them and I gather up the best of their comments and present them at the end of my report.

After I finished, Janice bid me to sit behind her. Since I have never been asked to do this before, I was glad to oblige although I would have done it anyway. The business of the court seemed pretty routine but I was attentive for several hours. There were mortal jurisdictional disputes that had been referred to local Metropolitans and a few mortal appeals for trading or transport rights which had been passed up to the Over-Lord because they crossed the boundaries of the Metropolitans under her. As usual she showed great wisdom and compassion in every detail. About mid-day there was a lull in the proceedings and someone sent for refreshments and I was included. The cakes and drink that the Immortals like to eat are similar to the ones we like and I was glad to join in. About an hour after the refreshments a single angel arrived with a communication for Janice and her court. I was not asked to leave but I did not receive the communication which apparently went directly to their minds. As the angel departed without the need of a portal I overheard one of the Immortals on the Dais comment that he knew that angel as one from the Throne Room.

The Immortal to Janice's right spoke first. "How long do you think this will take, Janice?"

"I think we should plan to accomplish it in about six months."

They all nodded.

Janice continued, "Do not begin any new processes among the mortals. Just try to get them as firmly established as possible in the necessary functions and then concentrate on spiritual issues."

They all nodded.

Then Janice turned to me. "Tim, I have something very important that I want you to concentrate all your energies on for the next half year."

"Yes, Ma'am." I waited for more.

"I want you to publish a series of booklets about spiritual issues; things like personal love and loyalty to the Emperor and the need to get together and share this love and loyalty. It is fine if these writings are repetitive. We will publish them and spread them everywhere. Keep them fairly short, 5 to 6 pages in length. Use all of your titles and be very sure and firm."

"Yes, absolutely."

"Start as soon as you can."

"Yes. Perhaps I should go back to the residence and get started."

Janice kissed me on the check and touched my shoulder. Lucius stepped in front of me and opened a portal and I stepped through into my study at the residence. Elaine stayed with the Over-Lord. For the first time in years I felt needed and encouraged. I finished what I thought would be considered a good pamphlet before I went to bed in the early morning hours. I used a lot of material from the writings of May as she has always been a spiritual favorite and several of Merle's proclamations and, of course, some from Mother Anna herself with a brief commentary and admonition from myself at the end encouraging all mortals to renew their commitment to the Emperor for His righteous government and generous blessings. I signed it using all of my titles. Something special was going to happen on the earth and my work was to be a key ingredient. Perhaps many would answer the call and there would be a new day for my work.

[N.D.] I saw that young woman again today, Victoria, the daughter of the administrator Horace Maxwell. I had met her again at the Metropolitan's annual dinner last month. She had grown up since the previous time I had seen her. She is special, beautiful and still humble, not like most young women these days. Elaine has not expressed any interest in my marrying. Over the generations she has usually had a hand in the mating of the Keeper either male or female. It passed through my mind that perhaps I should ask Elaine. Then I had an idea for another pamphlet and busied myself with that.

I presented my first set of four publications today. I walked over to the Metropolitan's Dais, – I love the walk over. Almost all of the footpath is constantly abloom with many varieties of flowers – and got Elaine's attention. She motioned me forward. I tried not to attract the attention of the Metropolitan but was unsuccessful.

"Young Tim." He always called me "young Tim."

"Excellency," I responded respectfully but firmly.

"You have some publications?"

I was surprised and pleased that my work was known as important to all the Immortals.

"Yes, here. . . " I held them out and he took them from my hands.

The Metropolitan glanced through my work. "Excellent! Elaine, let's get these to the printers right away." Elaine took them from his hand and gave them to one of her angel aides who promptly vanished to deliver them to the Metropolitan's mortal printing offices. The Metropolitan began conversing with someone else and I must have looked somewhat perplexed as to what to do next; so Elaine came over and took my arm and we took a stroll together. I thought 'if only she were still mortal, what a wonderful mate she would make.' I was suddenly afraid that she would know what I was thinking so I cleared my mind. She smiled up at me very sweetly. I waited.

"Tim. I am proud of you. Is there anything that you need to ask."

I should have known. "Yes, Elaine, actually there is. There is a young woman, Victoria Maxwell."

"You find her attractive?"

"Yes. Is there any reason . . ."

Elaine interrupted. "No, if you are attracted to her you may proceed. But, perhaps it would be best to wait until this special project is farther along." She looked up gently again.

"Good, I will delay."

She smiled in approval.

I made it a goal to produce four compelling pamphlets every two weeks. I would research and summarize every inspiring source that I could find and polish my writing to a high shine.

[N.D.] The semiautonomous civil magistrate had been dissolved due to corruption during Merle's time. About 14 years before Aunt Kathryn died a new civil assistant program had been put in place by the Metropolitans. These assistants are little more than message carriers for the local under-governors who actually do the judging in the world. I do not know why the Metropolitans have instituted such a program. Perhaps they are considering allowing a civil magistrate once again, or perhaps they are not. I yield to their wisdom.

I suppose my closest mortal friend is Aubrey McKinnon. He is the son of the civil assistant in Metropolitan Henry Sawyer's principality. Aubrey is a student of human nature and is a help to his father. This is not merely because he is his son. Aubrey is quite accomplished in his studies. My other close friends are James Warton, Matthew Anderson and Mary McDaniels. Mary is about the same age as I and also unmarried but we are only friends.

Aubrey doesn't miss anything. James is always joking. Matthew is very loyal. Mary is always fair. I am most often seen in public with them. They show a respectful deference to me in public. In private we are simply friends and equals. We can be found in various eating establishments more than once a week. Matthew will always get the table using my name.

"This place for himself," Matthew will hold my chair.

We order our food and talk quietly. Occasionally someone will notice me and look in my direction. I try to be responsive and nod to them. Lately, we have begun to notice a changing attitude. One evening several young men a few tables away had obviously had too much wine. My friends and I take only unfermented drinks in public or private.

"To the Emperor." One raised his glass.

"Yes, the Emperor. What good is he?"

"Shhhh, don't be a fool."

"The Emperor, Emperor Useless."

"Not you too? Be quiet!"

"The Emperor, who needs him."

"Shame to the Emperor."

Matthew started to rise. I touched his arm.

The manager came with some large helpers and put them out.

We all sat in silence.

Not only had they said these things in a public place but they had said them in my presence, knowing my office. Things are changing. No wonder the concern at court. I wondered why no angels appeared. Why didn't the Metropolitan deal with this treason? We left early that evening.

The next morning I sent Lucius to fetch Aubrey. I thought that I could enlist his help in understanding the current attitude. I thought of going to Elaine and I am not quite sure why I did not. For one thing I thought that surely she must know what was going on and she would tell me what she could if she wanted to. Also, this was a mortal problem and I wanted an informed mortal opinion of what, if anything, I could do to help. Aubrey and his father would know whatever a mortal could know.

"Wa. . .oh!" Aubrey exclaimed when he arrived at the residence. "Now that is some way to travel. I have never done that before."

In my concern I had sent Lucius without thinking that this would be a new experience to Aubrey.

"Yes, sorry old man. I didn't think. I need your help concerning this rebellion, you and your father."

"I talked to Dad about it last night. He says that this kind of thing has been going on for some time now."

"How long?"

"Several months."

"Can I get with him?"

"Yes, send Lucius. I want to see his reaction."

"No, he is the assistant. I will go to him."

"That will set a precedent."

"I know. But this is important. Will you get me an appointment with him?"

"Sure. How do I get back?"

"Lucius will take you," I conceded.

Lucius returned with a message. The assistant was waiting to see me. I returned with him immediately to his private office.

"Sir, I am honored." Assistant McKinnon said. He rose when I arrived and bowed his head briefly. Aubrey stood next to him looking quite serious. The assistant was tall and slim, much taller and slimmer than Aubrey. His blonde hair was graying and he had penetrating eyes. I could see a lot of him in Aubrey, especially around the eyes.

"It is my pleasure, sir," I answered. "We need to talk. We need to be very frank with each other." He nodded in agreement.

I learned from the assistant that he had been dealing with countless cases of disrespect and even sedition among the mortal populace. It apparently had begun about seven months ago. At first there was just a subtle lack of enthusiasm for the Emperor. Then people started acting like they did not care about his benevolent rule. Then there were semi-secret meetings to discuss living apart from his sovereign rule. Assistants were approached for help in this. Some assistants were going over to this rebellion saying that the arrangement brokered by my ancestor Mark was too weak. Why should we be in bondage to the Princes of this world? Mortals had put up with this long enough. Assistant McKinnon assured me that he was totally opposed to this rebellion, that he loves the Emperor and is totally loyal. He is himself meeting with other assistants who remain loyal.

"If you have been reporting to the Metropolitan, I doubt that the disloyal assistants have done the same. Or they are presenting false reports," I said.

"Yes, probably false reports."

"How can they imagine that the Immortals won't know the truth?"

"I don't know. The greater question is, why has there been no response from the Princes?"

'True, that is the important question." I resolved then and there that I would have to go to Elaine.

We talked some more and ate together. I liked the assistant almost as much as I liked Aubrey and I was convinced that they were absolutely loyal to the Emperor. As soon as I was back to my residence, I sent Lucius to ask for an appointment with Elaine. He was gone a long time, nearly four hours. By the time he returned I was anxious and had done little on my current pamphlets. Lucius took me to her.

"Dear Tim." She hugged me. When she saw the expression on my face, she bid me sit down and she sat opposite.

"Elaine, it is so upsetting. Surely you know. The McKinnons are totally loyal."

"Mark, just do what you can. Intensify your efforts to communicate the goodness of the Emperor to the people."

"I will, but surely He has not lost control. That would be impossible. I mean, what . . ."

She raised her hand. I stopped talking. "Of course He has not. We have not. However, we want to see just how far they will go. This is important."

"So I just continue?"

"Yes, work very hard. Lucius will give some extra help. And," She paused. "another Immortal has been assigned to work with you and me on this. I know that this is quite unusual. I am still the Legate, but Joseph has a good deal of experience in such things."

"Fine," I said.

"He will come to you," Elaine said. "He is off world right now but he will return shortly."

"Beyond the veil?"

"No, off world."

"I see." At least I thought I understood. He was on another world as William had indicated they could do to Joan.

"Lucius will know when he is coming."

"Good. What do I tell McKinnon?" I asked.

"Tell him to just keep doing the right thing and not to worry."

"Fine. I feel much better having talked to you, Elaine."

She took my hand with both of hers and pressed firmly. I was reassured but not happy. I had never expected such things to come to pass.

09.13.951 C.R.   Lucius did not have to inform me the next morning when the Immortal Joseph arrived. I was sitting near my study window when out of the corner of my eye I noticed a very large escort. No sooner had I turned to take a better look when they winked out of sight. I estimate that it was at least as large as an escort of an Over Lord, maybe larger. I hurried to my reception room as my private study is so small and cluttered. In the reception room stood a small man and an angel who is not at all like Lucius. He was at least as great as Raphael. Lucius stood beside him. I was once again thankful that they are on our side. I greeted Joseph with the utmost respect. Looking into his eyes I was aware of a gentle man who knew exactly what he was doing. He was no doubt capable of considerable sternness as well as great gentleness. He wore the same white garment that most Immortals wear. He had an unusual broad necklace which seemed to be attached like a collar to his robe. It was made of many flat yellow, blue, red and orange stones which are not transparent. There was some writing on it that resembled some hieroglyphs that I have seen in books, a definite Egyptian appearance. It hit me within the first few seconds who he was. I had researched every Joseph who was a ruler at any level during this Reign and found their pictures as well. I quickly eliminated these possibilities. The Joseph before me was not a ruler anywhere in the Reign of the Emperor on earth. This Joseph had to be the ancient son of Jacob who ruled in First Testament times under Pharaoh in ancient Egypt. His father, Jacob, was the father of the Emperor's ancestor Judah. I could not tell if his necklace referred to those ancient times or if it had something to do with his present off world position or some combination of both. I was definitely curious, but I would proceed slowly.

'It is such a great honor to have your Excellency at my residence," I said. I always started with the utmost of respect and formality and waited for the Immortals to give me leave to be less formal. This had the effect that I had hoped for.

"Please call me Joseph, Keeper Tim. I am here to help."

"Thank you, Joseph. I welcome your help and wisdom." I motioned towards some chairs and sent for refreshment through my steward, a mortal who stood very cautiously just outside the doorway.

On his way to the seat Joseph looked towards his magnificent angel and pointed to the corner of the room.

"Zebuleon," Joseph said. The angel repositioned and Lucius followed like a puppy. I was tempted to give Lucius an order but quickly decided to pass on that.

"I am sure you are fully aware of what has been happening," I said.

"I have been briefed," Joseph answered.

"I never dreamed that things could get so far out of line," I said. I am concerned for the dignity of my office, but more importantly, the Emperor is being disrespected."

"He knows this, Tim."

I shook my head in unbelief.

"I am going to tell you something that I believe you need to know," Joseph said.

" Mankind's final testing is about to take place. For almost a thousand years various rebellions, some of which have been reported, have occurred. This has proven that mortals still have a rebellious tendency, at least some of them. But now the ancient rebellious cherub will be loosed again for a short season. Many mortals will follow him and prove the righteousness of the Emperor, His Father and The Presence. You will need to walk this out with wisdom and patience so we can see those who will follow you and not the evil cherub."

I was overwhelmed. Why me?

"Your whole line has existed for this time, Tim. You are the man for your time. You will know what to do, Tim. Do not be afraid. I bring you the 'Presence'."

He touched my forehead. I felt the "Presence." It is awesome.

"And I will stay with you as long as I can." Joseph said.

Truthfully, I did not want to know right now what "as long as" really meant. I worked day and night and Lucius somehow got every pamphlet published almost immediately and distributed. There must have been angels involved in the process. The mortal organization could not have accomplished this so fast. In my new found fervor I write like I have never written before. I present my research and explain everything very clearly sometimes changing a single word or phrase eight or nine times before I am satisfied. Then I urge and implore all to listen and act accordingly. I feel that my writing has moved to a whole new level. My friends agree. I am making every effort to bring about change. Perhaps this is the sole reason for my being in this position. My feeling of calling is very high and I stay very busy. I have been thankful many times that I do not have family responsibilities to take me away from my work. But there is no way to really tell what effect my work is having.

I have asked Elaine if I can travel with Lucius and speak in many places in a continuing effort to convince my fellow mortals to increase their loyalty to our wonderful Emperor. Elaine said that she would have to ask the Over-Lord and would get back to me. The next day Elaine arrived at my residence without her escort. The portal opened in my study and I hastened to greet her. She took my hand right away and led me to sit next to her. There was a look in her eyes that I had never seen before.

"Tim, you have permission to make your trip."

"Thank you, Mistress. . . Elaine."

"Lucius will take you anywhere you wish to go and help you in any way that is needed."

"Good. I have been studying Mark's world tour. I believe that I would like to follow that pattern."

"That should work well."

"What should I do about the arrangements? Leave them to Lucius?"

" I will help. Give us a day or so and we will get it all set for you."

"Yes, thank you, thank you so much, dear Elaine."

I had never been sure if Immortals could cry, but I saw tears in Elaine's eyes and her brow was furrowed.

"What is it?" I asked.

She took my right hand in both of hers again.

"Tim, always, always know that I love you dearly."

"I do mistress. And I love you."

One more squeeze of my hand and she stood to leave. Lucius opened a portal for her and went with her. It seemed that my world was falling apart.

I soon learned that every Governor, Metropolitan, Over-Lord, and Viceroy along the extent of my trip had issued a general call for an assembly upon my arrival. There were enormous crowds. If I had not been aware of the extent of the problem, I would have shrunk from the task.

I wore Mark's robe and I even got a new red belt to wear with it as it symbolized my position as the mortal Spiritual Primate of the Empire. I used every honest device to make my case. I referred to the history of the Emperor from the time that he came as a man through the Glorious Return up to the present day. I reminded everyone that we have all lived in peace and prosperity under his righteous Reign. I spent hours talking of the wonderful lives we are all privileged to live. Violence and wrong doing are almost non-existent. There is always enough food and good accommodations for everyone since the Glorious Return. I told them how things had been before the present Reign and stressed that we should be thankful for every benefit. I reminded all that the Immortals healed our injuries and the few diseases that occurred among us. I expressed my own loyalty to the Emperor and briefly recited the history of my family from Anna to myself. Everywhere there was much applause and cheering. I began to wonder if there really was a problem.

I learned little from the Immortals that I encountered along the way. One of the few things that I found out was that the Emperor was seldom seen outside of Jerusalem in recent times. And even in Jerusalem he was more often on the Immortal side of the portal around the Throne than the mortal side. Was He withdrawing? Why? I soldiered on.

After about two months we returned home and I slept for three days. Since Lucius did not require sleep, he would just hang around. I remember during the few times that I was awake seeing him standing there. After I recovered, I wanted to see Aubrey and Assistant McKinnon. I sent Lucius for them. Next I intended to see Elaine.

Assistant McKinnon said that according to reports that he had heard my trip had had a generally positive effect. However, the number of cases of disloyalty to the Emperor had not declined greatly. Aubrey said that he did not understand this behavior. As a behaviorist it did not make sense for people to rebel when everything is so good. They both shook their heads. I had Lucius return them to their home. Aubrey was excited about that again. I was very sleepy so I retired early.

That night I had the most wonderful dream. In this dream I could see myself lying in my bed at the residence, my mouth wide open and snoring as I usually do. Sometimes, I even wake myself. At the same time I was standing in one of the side chambers of the Temple in

Jerusalem. These chambers seemed to be used for meetings, sometimes meetings between mortals and Immortals or between mortals and angels. A magnificent angel appeared before me. He was very tall with the same large head that Gabriel has. He also had those same piercing eyes. I presumed him to be a member of the Powers Choir and I addressed him with respect but not fear. I do not fear the Emperor's angels.

"An Angelic Power." I said certainly.

"No, Keeper, I am a Vicar. My name is Aker. You must come and confer with me."

"Confer?"

"Yes, we must talk."

"Good, fine. In the morning I will come to you."

"I await," he answered.

Then the dream was over. I slept through the rest of the night but when I awakened, I remembered the dream clearly.

I sent Lucius immediately to ask Elaine if I could talk to her as soon as possible. She came to me. I told her about my dream and she smiled.

"Is it alright to go?" I asked. "Does this constitute a summons to the capital?"

"Yes, I believe that it does," she said.

"Will you go?" I asked.

"That is not necessary. Lucius will take you. Tell him when you are ready and brief me when you return." She smiled and touched my shoulder and was gone.

Lucius and I found ourselves in that same side chamber in the Temple in Jerusalem. I had never actually been inside the Temple although there were likenesses of it around the residence at home as well as ones of the Palace and other parts of the Imperial city undoubtedly put there by May generations ago. Lucius remained with me and visible. In a few minutes Aker arrived. He was more impressive in person than in the dream. My heart did skip a beat. Lucius bowed deeply.

"We were obliged to meet here," he said, "because no one from my rank has appeared in this world before. Your residence is not secure."

What did he mean by that?

He continued. "The Temple is always a safe place. It is the blessed duty of my Rank to increase loyalty among mortals. We are seldom visible. We attempt to inspire and promote loyalty in every way possible."

I nodded.

"Your time as Keeper will be the most difficult that any Keeper has ever had."

I gulped.

"All mortals who have loyalty are going to need much encouragement. Those who desire loyalty will need help to grow into it. All those without it will be marked for judgment. Do you understand?"

"Yes," I answered. "How do we proceed."

"My Lord, the great Raphael, has instructed me according to the directions given him by the Worshipper Seth."

I suddenly realized that we had just jumped another two Ranks neither of which had ever been seen on earth. I also knew from my studies in the writings of May and Merle that the Seraphs and Cherubs never left the presence of the Emperor's Father. The Worshippers were the connection between things which were totally heavenly and the things that have earthly or mortal consequences. My heart had jumped at the thought of a Prince. Now a Worshipper was in the picture.

Aker continued, "We are instructed to do all that we can to encourage all mortals to grow in loyalty at this crucial time."

"I have sensed that it is crucial," I interrupted, "can you tell me more?"

"Only that time is growing short, very short. Enormous changes are in store not only for the mortals but for the earth and the heavens as well. Even we are not told everything. Check your ancient writings."

I nodded.

"Your traveling has just begun. You are to travel again to as many cities and territories as you can. This angel will transport you as usual. You are to study the ancient writings, especially those of your predecessor, the Keeper May. This time you are to speak to the mortals about increasing in virtue as well as in loyalty to the Emperor. Of course, the Emperor is the supreme example of virtue, but you must illustrate from the lives of others as well so that your hearers will be more able to identify with your examples. Tell them that this may be their last chance to change. Tell them to make haste to change and to pray to the Emperor for help. Do you understand, Keeper Tim?"

"Yes, I understand." I could not explain why, but it all made perfect sense to me.

"I will work with you from beyond the veil," Aker continued. Do not be timid to push your agenda. I will remove obstacles and prepare the way for you. Be strong, Tim. Be courageous." He paused. "Now," he continued, "look around the Temple with me. Draw strength from it."

We walked together. The Temple is very special. There is a presence of the Emperor about it even when he is not there. Mortals are usually not allowed beyond the outer court so I was especially curious about being inside. A powerful yet gentle glow emanated from the back. Aker reminded me that that very light had once been used to lead the followers of the Emperor. But the "Presence," yes, "the Presence" was what was so overpowering. Yes, that was it.

"Aker," I asked anxiously.

"Yes."

He was a very grand and tall angel, but his voice had much kindness and patience in it. He was a Vicar after all.

"The 'Presence". Keeper Joan was once allowed the 'Presence' for several years. Is my mission now important enough for me to have the 'Presence' as well?"

He stopped. "Yes, Tim. It is. But you had to ask on your own initiative. The 'Presence' will be with you in this and you will be guided by him. He is the Brother of the Emperor."

All of Joan's report came flooding back into my mind.

"Come, walk with me towards the light," he said.

As we approached the wondrous light at the back of the Temple, it reflected more and more off of the golden walls and furniture. It became heavier and heavier, wonderful but heavy. I was determined to get as close as possible but I soon realized that I could not stand up under it for very long. Finally, I dropped to my knees and crawled for a short distance, then I completely collapsed under its glorious weight. I lay there for an undetermined amount of time. I saw Aker walk ahead deep into the glow and then he was gone. After what could have been hours or days I came to myself. I retraced my route crawling until I could stand and then I slowly backed away from the glow. I felt the "Presence" with me. I had never imagined how wonderful it could be.

Lucius took me directly home and I slept for days. Then one morning I awoke quite refreshed and sent Lucius to inquire of Elaine. She bid me come to her this time. We arrived in her receiving hall.

"Tim, welcome back. You got your commission?"

By that I presumed that she knew what Aker had wanted.

"Yes, it looks like I'm on the road again."

"Only this time, little brother, I will be with you."

"We will travel together?"

"Yes. You will be the speaker. But I will be with you to assure that everything goes as well as possible. This is no lack of confidence in you, Tim. It is the condition of the world and the mission itself. As a matter of fact, we will travel with my full escort."

"Wow. I guess that is about the highest priority mission that any Keeper has ever been given. It is a heavy load, Elaine."

"Yes, but you are up to it and I am behind you all the way. Tim, I have been the Imperial Legate responsible for the Keepers from Anna until you. I have loved each one of them as I love you. Their work has been my work. Your work is my work. Go back to your residence and instruct your staff that you will be gone almost constantly from now. Take a day or so. See your friends. Have Lucius bring you here when you are ready to go."

"Yes, Elaine. I will not be long. Lucius, to the residence."

01.16.954 C.R.   We visited every Dais in the world over the next two years. From each Dais we roamed the countryside speaking at gatherings. Every arrival at a Dais was a great event. Elaine's escort combined with that of each ruler giving almost the appearance of a Viceroys canopy. Every gathering away from a Dais was attended with Elaine's escort which is sizable in her capacity as Imperial Legate. Elaine introduced me every time and encouraged everyone to listen intently. Attendance was high and people seemed to respond. I urged the seeking of all the virtues and loyalty to the Emperor. I told them "whatsoever things are true, whatsoever things are honest, whatsoever things are just, whatsoever things are pure, whatsoever things are lovely, whatsoever things are of good report; think on these things and do only these. This is a day of testing. Your very lives and futures hang in the balance." I felt the "Presence" in all that I said and did. That part was wonderful.

11.19.954 C.R.   Then I received instructions from Elaine that if they had not come from her I would have not been able to believe them.

"Tell them, Tim, that the Emperor has promised openly that all those who seek virtue and are loyal to him will be eligible for the afterlife. This is something that has not been promised to mortals since the glorious return and the beginning of the reign."

I did as she told me, but I had one burning question on my mind. When we were back at the ruler's residence that evening, I asked her.

"Elaine."

"Yes, Tim."

"What if we do all of this and things keep getting worse. I will have failed. You people know a lot. The Emperor knows everything. Sometimes I am a little confused."

"First of all, Tim," she touched my arm. "You are not responsible for the success or failure of this mission. Neither am I. Ours is only to obey. If we are faithful, that is all that we can do. And yes, the Emperor does know everything. Mortal humanity itself is being tested in your generation. Left to their own, with the evil Cherub and his minions out of the way, mortals will show their true motives. That is the Emperor's purpose in this. It is important to Him and to His Father and to the 'Presence'. After it is all over, and it will be over, Tim, believe me, everything will change and I believe that you will see it all."

That was good enough for me.

10.09.983 C.R.   I awoke this morning to something most disturbing. Lucius is gone. At first I presumed that this was temporary. I have become so used to him and he has always conducted my affairs as Keeper. Generally if he is away for a short time, it is on an errand for me. I have never awakened to find him gone. After an hour I started to be genuinely concerned. After two hours I knew that it was serious.

[N.D.] I made my way to the Dais just as I had every morning for years. I knew that I was privileged to be a member of the court but I always felt at home nearest the Dais. When I arrived, there were about a dozen mortals there. There were no Immortals. Some of my fellow mortals seemed concerned. Such children, I thought. The Immortals are always in charge. They are all simply busy or "away" right now. Some more mortals arrived. An then some more. Hours passed. Soon it was evening. I joined the others in real concern. How could they all be away for so long? They did not require sleep. No angels were evident either. All of us began to feel a little lost. We had never known a time when the Immortals were all absent. This could not be their annual banquet because there was not even one Immortal at the Dais and it was not spring time. It was late in the summer. There were no angels anywhere. People started to come to the Dais to ask for help on one matter or another. We court mortals tried to assure them that the Immortals would be back soon and that all would be well. But still they did not come.

[N.D.] Weeks went by. The court mortals kept the Dais area clean and tidy. They checked with mortals in other jurisdictions. There did not seem to be any Immortals left on the continent. They wanted to check with mortals near Jerusalem but they did not have the means to do so. The Immortals and the angels had always handled distance communication. Many communities started sending pilgrims to Jerusalem to find out what was going on. Was the Emperor still on the throne? Aubrey believed that this was a test to see if people would follow the good things taught to mortals over the now almost 1,000 years of the Reign. People from different regions started not trusting each other and borders were guarded by mortals organizing themselves into guard groups. What was the world coming to?

[N.D.] Then one morning in the distance angels could be seen approaching our Dais. Later we learned that they had appeared on every Dais in the world at the same time. These angels were mighty and impressive but they were different than the ones that had always served the Immortals. The angels had always had a lingering aroma about them, something like that of the Immortals when they returned to sight. Elaine had always said it was like the smell of jasmine only better, stronger and sweeter. These angels did not smell like that. They smelled like sulfur fumes.

[N.D.] I remember my ancestress, Anna, writing in her personal dairy about seeing the Emperor. When this being appeared with so many angels, I wanted to see him. None of us had seen angels for so long and we were hungry to see someone who was not mortal like ourselves. We had all been confused for quite a long time.

Was this the emperor? An angel? Or at least a form of one? I did not want to see his eyes. From my place behind the chair I pulled back. Was this the light that Grandmother Anna had seen. She said that the light around the Emperor was bright and shinny but it did not hurt her eyes. She said that there was a sweet, sweet smell. This light was red, it was harsh and the air smelled of coals and sulfur. Who was this come back to us now? He did not stay long. He appointed one of his assistants to sit in the seat of the Metropolitan and left.

[N.D.] These new princes do not punish wicked acts, they seem to actually encouraged them. Also, there seems to be little agreement among the territorial princes. They seem to vie for power between themselves. Our new prince, one Gaol as he is named, sits proudly in the Metropolitan's seat and occasionally growls orders to those around him. There are five assistants seated on the Dais with him. The seat always reserved for the Emperor has been removed. All the angels have been replaced. Occasionally one of these angels appears with some poor mortal that has been caught in a wrong doing of some kind. The punishment seems to be meted out more on the basis of having been caught in the deed rather than in the fact that the deed was wrong. These princes have the power to execute as the old ones did, but they enjoy it more. They also enjoy tormenting the accused before they carry out the sentence. Sometimes a plaintiff is given charge of an area instead of being disciplined. Other princes visit from time to time and they use this time to brag about how they are expanding their territories. The ones that lose authority seem to move down in the ranks where they attempt to move up again by getting an advantage over a fellow prince and gaining the attention of their emperor. Mortal leaders under the influence of these dark leaders are raising armies and warring against each other. Everywhere there is misery and anarchy.

[N.D.] Along with these cruel angels have come the shadow people. They seem to have some relationship to the angels, but I do not understand how or why. The shadow people are not angels; they move across the earth as we do. They have a faint form. They form a distortion against a background that shimmers and presents an outline to the eye. They are almost transparent. At night they can be almost impossible to see. During the day it is easier, but they do not prefer to come out then. We do not know where they stay. They do like to hang around the Dais and be in contact with the cruel angels. They are of various sizes. Lately they have been seen around places where humans congregate to engage in unsavory activities, orgies and such. The angels do not seem to gather here. They are more into raw power. Some mortals who have come to us for help have been in places where these shadow people are commonly seen. They will cover the body of a mortal who is engaged in immortal activity with their own form; they seem to get a lot of enjoyment out of it. They are seen often at fights or battles. They examine every wound and seem gleeful when someone cries out in pain.

[N.D.]   I have examined some of the more uncommon ancients texts from the First Testament era and I believe I may have come up with a possible answer about the shadow people. It seems that some ancients believed that what we see as the shadow people were the offspring of the cruel angels. They believe that in very ancient times the cruel angels mated with evil mortal females who brought forth children who were giants in their day. Then there was a great flood of water that covered the entire earth and only eight people chosen by God escaped in a great ship with many pairs of animals. All the other mortals died and their souls went to the waiting place to await the appearance of the Emperor on the earth. The Emperor visited the waiting place and led the righteous out. The souls of the giants, however, did not go to the waiting place. Instead, the Prince Michael condemned these souls, our shadow people, to roam the earth until the end of all things. I believe that this must be the true account about these creatures. The only way that we have found to repel the shadow creatures when they come near us or our homes is to call on the name of the Emperor, our Emperor. They can not bear to hear the name of the Emperor in the familiar. So they run away and do not return for a long time.

[N.D.] I do not know why I have not been signaled out. After all, I am the heir of Anna. Maybe it is because I am seen as powerless and of no importance or influence these days with so little interest in the ancient texts.

Some of us mortals have started meeting in secret. We know that the punishment will most probably be death if we are caught but we care little about this. This new regime is corrupt and selfish. And they do not seem to be aware of everything that is happening like the good princes were. We get together and long for the return to better days. We share memories about the benevolent reign. There is even a renewed interest in the ancient texts and I am being asked to interpret in various groups. One young girl last week actually called me "your Excellency." We study the writings of Anna and the entire line down to myself.

Last evening we had a new visitor at the secret meeting. One of our most trusted members brought him. He is a man named Paul who has recently arrived from the western wars. He is the cousin of Kirk Feldon who has been meeting with us from the beginning. Because of this we were inclined to accept him at once. We have gotten overly cautious recently because some of our group has been detained by the local assistant. This judge is loyal to the local dark angel prince and is not friendly to our interests. Paul tells us that the new dark angel prince Metropolitan of Dallas is a great rival of the new dark angel Metropolitan of Houston. They have each promoted mortal generals to raise an army for battle. The generals hate each other and each rival prince. The army is gathered to satisfy the lust of the dark angel princes to see mortals kill each other in battle. It is a terrible sight. Men are challenged to fight bravely and may die in hand to hand combat. The dark angel princes on both side watch from the air and rally their generals to battle. The main problem is that nothing is offered the mortals for their bravery and effort. Many die to no promise of an afterlife and the battles never seem to end. The dark angel princes are never satisfied.

01.12.999 C.R.   In an effort to keep ahead of my disciples, I have been studying the ancient texts again and I discovered a possible answer to our situation. In the Second Testament of the Emperor which Anna preserved and commented on, an evil prince is mentioned. There is a reference that could be interpreted to fit our predicament. It seems that this prince is very old and evil. After the return of the Emperor he was bound away from mortals and from his power over territories on the earth that he should "deceive the nations no more." But after a thousand years of benevolent reign he is spoken about as being "loosed for a little season." Could this be it? If so, this evil reign can only last so long. Then what will come? I must study and meditate more to be as sure as I can. Others are counting on me to interpret correctly and to give them help and comfort. Oh, mother Anna, Joan, Aunt Kathryn, I wish you could help me be sure now. What I wouldn't give for just a few minutes right now with Elaine or even Lucius.

12.29.999 C.R.   About four in the morning I was awakened by a bright light coming through my window so I went outside. To the East I saw a glow and first thought that the sun was rising early. As we watched it began to grow, it was coming towards us.   I looked up to see an enormous ball of fire rolling across the land towards us. It was almost as wide as the Eastern horizon and almost as high as the clouds. I knew that none of us could survive this. As it rolled closer and closer, I fell to my knees thanking the Emperor that along with us this evil government would be destroyed. Instinctively I put my hands up to shield myself from this inferno. I could feel the heat on my face and hands as it approached. Then I felt the touch of a gentle hand on my back. I hoped that it was Elaine and it was. She smiled at me.

"Be at peace, Tim," she said, "this fire can not hurt you."

I wanted to believe that and I suddenly felt a strange tingle all over my body. I looked down at my hands. They looked the same. By then the fireball was upon us. We were totally immersed in it. Elaine was on my right and Lucius appeared on my left. I was so glad to see them I almost forgot to be afraid. The flames did not burn us although it consumed every natural thing around us even the rocks.

"This fire will consume the old earth and all the evil," Elaine said. This is the beginning of the new earth and the new heavens."

www.ingramcontent.com/pod-product-compliance
Lightning Source LLC
Chambersburg PA
CBHW030330030726
47499CB00003B/710